LocoThology
2013

Tales of Fantasy and Science Fiction

I0622344

Loconeal Publishing
Amherst

LocoThology
2013
Tales of Fantasy and Science Fiction

This book is a work of fiction. The names, characters, places, and events in this novel are either fictitious or are used fictitiously. Any resemblance to actual events or persons is entirely coincidental.

Table of Contents

Soul Pirates

by Sandra Wickham

What the hell was her stepmother up to now? Breanne dodged the junk-removal truck parked in their driveway and entered the house through the side door.

The house smelled weird, like paint fumes. "Dad?"

He was probably at work. She shouldn't have expected him to be home to greet her just because she'd been at her grandmother's for a week. Probably forgot she was coming home today.

Holy shit. The paint smell was coming from her room. She dropped her bags, ran down the hall and skidded to a halt in the open doorway.

It was all gone. The crow's nest hideout with climbing ropes, the pirate ship's wheel on its standing base and worst of all, the dark-stained pirate ship bunk bed including the ladder, ship rails and mini quarter deck headboard. Breanne's mother had made all of it.

Sharyl, her stepmother, stood by the far wall of her room, paint roller in hand. Gone was the mural of an island of palm trees surrounded by turquoise water, the full moon in a dark-blue sky shining down on a pirate ship in full sail. Now an annoying violet color covered every wall.

First, came disbelief. Next, a shroud of darkness weighed down on her, her heart pushed to the pit of her stomach. Tears filled her eyes, but she willed them away, determined not to give her stepmother the satisfaction of seeing her cry. Sharyl had moved the remaining furniture away from the walls. Breanne could see her mother's spell book now sticking out from under her only remaining chair.

"What did you do?"

"What? You're too old for that stuff. Plus, you'll be out of the house in a year, and this will become my new work room."

Breanne knew she couldn't stay, but she wasn't prepared to face that yet. She wanted to go to university and become an architect like her mother. Breanne lunged forward, grabbed the spell book and rushed back out the kitchen door to try to catch the junk truck. Maybe she could reassemble the room herself.

She stepped out onto the driveway in time to see the Junk Removal sign on the back of the truck as it drove away. That was it. She sank to the ground and let the tears flow, hugging her mother's spell book to her chest. Cross-legged on the driveway, she missed her mother so much it hurt. Another thought crept in, and she let out a gasp. With everything destroyed, the portal would be unprotected. Things were about to get really messed up.

Breanne's mother had built the pirate room to protect the portal and had taught her to defend their house and their world from the Soul Pirates. The original memories were faint, but she remembered wispy shapes, red glowing eyes and sunken faces. Her most vivid recollection was of her mother chasing them away.

When Breanne was older, her mother explained how her powers drew the Soul Pirates, but she'd managed to fight them off. Now, for the same reasons, they were attracted to Breanne, and despite her mother's efforts, they'd found her. Instead of running, they'd built the pirate room and her mother had cast spells over it.

When the pirates tried to come through, either Breanne or her mother would feel it and have to go sit on the pirate bed. The room around them disappeared. The sounds and smells of the open sea filled their senses, and they found themselves on the deck of the ship painted in the mural on the wall. Breanne didn't know where their crew came from, but they were always there with them, competent and ready to heed orders to fight off the incoming Soul Pirates. They'd never had to get close enough to see the Soul Pirates' faces, but their red eyes still haunted her dreams.

Eventually the Soul Pirates gave up. They hadn't tried to cross over since her mother died four years ago. Her father didn't know anything, never suspected, and no one who came to their house ever thought twice about her pirate-themed room. After her mother's death no one had even suggested getting rid of it. Until now. Her idiot stepmother had destroyed it, and they would all end up dead, their souls devoured.

"Get your shit together," Breanne whispered to herself. She pushed to her feet as her father pulled into the driveway. He'd been allowed to live in blissful ignorance because her mother had thought it best, but Breanne disagreed. It was time he knew what had been going on and what Sharyl had done.

Her father slammed the car door. "Hey, sweetheart. How was Grandma's?"

Breanne clutched the spell book in one arm. "Dad, we have to talk."

He blinked then nodded and held an arm out toward the side door. "Okay, let's go inside."

Breanne grabbed his wrist. "No, it has to be out here."

Her father sighed. It looked as though a weight fell on him. "This is about Sharyl again, isn't it?"

"She completely demolished my room, took down all Mom's pirate stuff and sent it to the junkyard. Did you know she was going to do that?"

Her father shrunk a little more. "No, I didn't know about it. But, I'm sure you two will design a great new room for you."

Breanne clenched her teeth then forced herself to take a deep breath. "No, we won't. She's already making it into her new work room."

He put his hand on her shoulder. "I know you've been upset by the changes Sharyl has made, but it's her way of feeling comfortable here."

She dropped her grip on his wrist. "You mean like when she got rid of our family cat? Or do you mean when she got rid of anything and everything Mom ever touched?"

Her father shook his head. "I know it's not easy for you—"

"It's more complicated than that," she cut him off.

"I understand you loved the room your Mom built, but maybe it is time to move on. You're a little old for pirates, aren't you?"

She should've known he'd stick up for Sharyl. "Forget it." She turned and went inside without looking back. She was on her own.

Later that afternoon a new bed with a plain wooden frame arrived, and Breanne stayed out of the way while Sharyl directed where it should go. Breanne had bigger things to worry about. Her body tingled in anticipation of the next Soul Pirate attack. What was she going to do? Maybe she could offer up Sharyl's soul and they'd take it and leave. While that thought amused her, she knew it didn't work that way. The pirates wouldn't stop with one soul. They'd plunder and pillage every soul they could find. After her family, they'd move on to her entire neighborhood and beyond. She had to stop them.

Her stomach tightened and her skin flared with heat. The sensations meant the Pirates were attempting to cross over. Breanne ran to her room. The house shook.

Sharyl dropped the book she'd been about to place on the shelf and her eyes went wide. "It's an earthquake."

Breanne was about to snap at her that it wasn't an earthquake, then stopped herself. It'd be easier to let both Sharyl and her dad think it was an earthquake than trying to explain what was really going on.

Sharyl turned to her, eyes serious. "We need to get to the basement."

"You go, I'm right behind you." It was a small lie, but Sharyl didn't fall for it.

"I mean it, young lady—" Her mouth hung open, but no more words came out. Water seeped from the walls. They were coming. Without the spelled ship furniture, there was nothing to stop them entering.

Breanne stood in the middle of the room and flipped through the spell book. She'd been meaning to study her mom's spell book, but every time she took it out, the memories hurt too much. Most of it she couldn't decipher, made up of unfamiliar words, symbols and pictograms. There'd been no need. They'd been safe.

Sharyl stood frozen, staring at the water coming through the walls. "What . . . ." She stepped forward and reached a hand toward it.

"No," Breanne yelled and lunged forward. It was too late. The wall transformed into a waterfall of gushing water.

Sharyl let out a whooping scream and back-pedaled away from the wall.

"What's going on?" Her father ran into the room. The water spilled out into the hall behind him.

"Soul pirates," Breanne shouted over the sound of the rushing water. It was cold and moving quickly up past her ankles. "Mom made my pirate room to hold them off." She heard Sharyl let out a gasp, but Breanne ignored it. She held up the spell book to her father's face. "It's in here." She lowered the book and her eyes. "I just don't know how to do it."

As she expected, he looked at her like she was crazy. He grabbed her arm and waved at Sharyl who started toward them. "Let's go."

Breanne pulled away from her father, ran by Sharyl and stood in the middle of the room. The water rushed in as she flipped through the spell book, reading her mother's hand written notes in the margins.

She jabbed a page. "Got something."

Her mother had scribbled Pirates at the top and a translation above each symbol for the entire spell. Maybe she'd done it for Breanne?

Ignoring her father and Sharyl, she took a deep breath and stepped to the wall. Holding the book in front of her like a shield, she yelled the words at the pouring water. From the very first line of the spell, she felt the magic flowing through her. It felt the same when she'd ridden the pirate bed into the other realm. With a newfound confidence, she finished the last words and focused on the wall.

The water stopped. Breanne glanced over at her father and stepmother. They both stared at the wall, watching Sharyl's new paint streaking in drippy lines.

Sharyl backed up to the new bed and sat down on the mattress still wrapped in plastic. "It must have been some sort of leak in the pipes."

Stunned, Breanne looked at her father then back at Sharyl. Was she for real? "It wasn't the pipes!" Then realized how freaked out she sounded. Screw it. She was freaked out. "All I did was hold them off for a bit. It won't last long. They'll be back."

Her father stepped toward her, quickly. "What do you mean? What's this nonsense about your mother and your pirate room?"

Breanne had never stood up to her father, not only because she was his daughter and was supposed to do what he said, but because she adored him. When her mother had died and it had just been the two of them, he'd been more than strong enough for both of them. This time she had to stand her ground.

"Dad, you loved mom. You were together for almost twenty years. I can't believe you didn't know something was different about her."

The plastic creaked under Sharyl as she shifted around, but Breanne kept focused on her father. "Things happened around her, didn't they? Not always good things, either. But she got herself out of it, until the last time."

His eyes sort of glazed over, as if he'd gone somewhere far away. He nodded and blinked back tears. "I guess I knew, but she didn't want to share it with me."

Breanne reached out to touch her dad's arm. "She just wanted to protect you."

He looked in her eyes and they both knew what the other was thinking. Neither of them had been able to protect Breanne's mother in the end.

Her father got Sharyl to her feet. "We all need to go."

Breanne stared up at him. "No, Dad. I need to do something."

He looked at Sharyl, then back at Breanne. "I'm not leaving you."

"Good. Maybe you can help me." Her brain raced in circles, always coming back to the same thing. "We need a boat."

"A boat?"

Breanne paced her now unfamiliar room. "Something that could work as a boat. It doesn't have to actually float. I have the spell in here."

Her father stepped in front of her, stopping her. "What do you plan to do with the boat?"

There was far too much to explain. "I need to find our crew so we can fight off the Soul Pirates." She knew how bizarre it sounded, but she didn't like the look on her father's face. She felt it too. Doubt. How could she face them alone?

Her father must've seen it cross her face. He put his hands on both her shoulders. "You're just like her, you know. If she could do it, so can you."

Breanne met his eyes and felt tears fill hers. Since when did her father have any faith her? No time for that now.

Breanne spun toward the bed. "Maybe we could use that." She got her hands under the mattress and tried to lift it out of the frame.

Her dad grabbed the other end. Together they threw the mattress aside and flipped the frame over.

"How's this work?" he asked her.

She shrugged and looked around for the spell book. Where had she put it when she'd flipped the bed?

"Looking for this?" Sharyl held the spell book, disgust on her face.

Breanne's heart went hard. "Give it to me."

Sharyl didn't take her eyes off the book. "This was your mother's." It was a statement, not a question.

Breanne moved toward her, hand held out. "You need to give

that to me now."

Sharyl met Breanne's gaze then tucked the book into the crook of her arm. "Your mother made herself insane. I can't allow you to throw your life away." She started for the door.

Breanne's body flushed with heat. Her mother hadn't gone insane. She'd taken on evil spirits in order to save the twins next door. It had been too much for her. After struggling for months against them, she'd died.

Breanne turned to her father, but she recognized the look on his face. It was the same one he got every time he was torn between his new wife and his daughter.

Breanne ran behind Sharyl and grabbed the book from under her arm. Sharyl held on with her other hand and spun around so they were in a tug of war.

"Stay out of this," Breanne yelled as she yanked on the book.

"I'm in it, whether you want me here or not."

Sharyl's eyes went to the wall and she let out a cry. Within the wall, a swirling vortex of dark grey mist pulled at them. Breanne's breath locked in her chest as red eyes flashed behind the mist.

"What is that?" Sharyl's voice shook.

"You need to give me the book, now." Breanne tried to keep her voice calm, but she was screaming on the inside. The eyes now had skulls to go with them, and the tip of a sword thrust through the wall.

Sharyl looked down at the spell book once more then handed it over.

Breanne let out the breath she didn't know she'd been holding and found the pirate pages marked with her mother's notes. Without looking away from the book, she stepped over the bed frame's edge and into their makeshift boat. Out of the corner of her eyes, she saw her father get in as well. She met his eyes, and he nodded at her. To her surprise, Sharyl also stepped into the boat.

"What?" She gave Breanne a weak smile. "I'm coming too."

Breanne didn't have time to argue. The swirling grey mass on the wall grew by the second. "Everybody, sit."

Being a single bed, it was a tight fit, but they managed it. Calling on all her magic, Breanne spoke the words in the spell book. "Close your eyes," she instructed after she was almost finished. "And maybe hold on." She finished the final line of the spell.

Her room disappeared, and they were floating on the dark waters just beyond the familiar island with its blowing palm trees, the smell of saltwater all around. They were in a rowboat, thankfully bigger than her bed. In the distance she spotted the ship they used to sail on. Unfortunately, the Soul Pirate ship was closer, its black and white skull flag clearly visible as it charged toward them.

Sharyl looked a little green.

Her father sat upright, adjusting quickly to the rocking of the boat. "Now what?"

Breanne had to shrug. "I'm not really sure. We need them to come help us," She pointed out beyond the pirates to her old ship. "Before the Soul Pirates get to us."

It was clear that wasn't going to happen. In fact, the Soul Pirate ship was almost on top of them. Before they came up alongside the rowboat, one wispy Soul Pirate skeleton jumped from the ship's rail. It landed without a sound into the middle of the rowboat.

It pointed its sword at Sharyl. Breanne took a deep breath and put herself in front of her stepmother. She might not get along with Sharyl, but she made her father happy. That was enough.

The pirate's red eyes flared. He rotated his body and stabbed her father instead.

"No!" Breanne lunged at the pirate, but fell through its body. She slammed her hands into the bottom of the bed and pain sparked up her arms. She pushed herself up and turned back. A willowy white light danced up from her father's chest into the pirate's embedded sword and up the pirate's arm. The pirate's skeleton jaw gaped wide as the light approached it.

Movement above caught Breanne's eye. A seagull appeared through the mist, and immediately Breanne realized it was her mother. It landed on the rail beside her and Breanne knew she needed to dig deeper for more power.

With a scream of rage, she lunged at the Soul Pirate. This time, she didn't go through him. His body felt as solid as any human. She pushed him over the edge of their boat. The sword pulled from her father and he gasped for breath. There was no splash when the pirate hit the water, but he disappeared into the dark depths nonetheless.

Breanne wanted to say a million things to her mother, but she flew away to their old ship. Seconds later, it engaged the Soul Pirate ship in a full-on battle.

"Paddle!" Breanne thrust her hands into the water to get them away from the fighting. Her father and Sharyl joined in. They barely got out of the way before explosions tore through the belly of the Soul Pirate ship. The ship sank into the ocean.

Her father punched his fists into the air and let out a cheer like a little kid. Breanne couldn't help but grin at him. She knew, though, it wasn't the end. They would come back. The victorious ship pulled up alongside them.

Her crew crowded along the rail, including the seagull, her mother.

"We're here for ya," one with an eye patch said. He gave her a wink. Or it might have been a blink, since she couldn't see his other eye. "Ready and waiting."

"Thank you." Breanne realized she might never be able to leave their house, might never be able to go on to have her own life.

Her mother flew down and settled on the rail of the little rowboat.

Breanne sat to match the bird's height. "I don't understand what you're doing here."

"I'm here for you," came the answer, though the beak hadn't

moved. Breanne flashed a look at her father and Sharyl, but could tell by their faces she was the only one who heard her mother. "I'm proud of you," her mother went on. "I couldn't have come here without you."

Breanne sniffed back tears and couldn't find her voice, so she only nodded. She felt her father take her hand.

"You'll be fine," her mother's voice told her. "You're stronger than I ever was. This proves it. There's a spell in my book that you can use to make sure the pirates follow you and don't bother anyone else. You'll have to fight them if they do come back, but I know you can do it."

"I don't know if I can. Will you always come help me?" Breanne wished it wasn't a damn bird she was talking to. She wanted her mother in her body, to wrap her arms around her.

"You can and you will. I can't come again, but I'll always be with you. I love you."

With that, she extended her wings, lifted off from the boat and flew away, disappearing into the midnight sky.

Sharyl let out a relieved sigh. "Can we go home now?"

Breanne nodded. "Yes we can. Just close your eyes."

Breanne repeated the spell to take them back again. Fresh tears for the loss of her mother trickled down her face, but at the same time, she'd never felt closer to her. The Soul Pirates wouldn't quit, but neither would she.

About the Author:

Sandra Wickham lives in Vancouver, Canada with her husband and two cats. Her friends call her a needle crafting aficionado, health guru and ninja-in-training. Sandra's short stories have appeared in Evolve, Vampires of the New Undead, Evolve, Vampires of the Future Undead, Chronicles of the Order, Crossed Genres magazine and The Urban Green Man. She blogs about writing with the Inkpunks, is the Fitness Nerd columnist for the Functional Nerds and reads slush for Lightspeed Magazine.

Obituary of "Pirate" Samuel Tree, Aged 3

by Michael Donoghue

Obituary—The Economist—June 14, 2064

"Pirate" Samuel Tree

Samuel Tree, one of the world's most infamous and blatantly unrepentant pirates, died today, aged three.

"Pirate" Samuel Tree—as he became internationally known—was delivered on April 2nd, 2061, in Ohio's Holmes County, in the world's last Amish community. Samuel Tree was unique. Born without any gene screening, modification or augmentation, he was completely organic. Had he lived to adulthood, he would have faced a life filled with barriers and challenges due to this disability.

Despite his crippled nature he remained a happy toddler with blonde curly hair, a toothy smile and a keen sense of exploration. Nevertheless, registering Samuel's GeneTag revealed the tragedy.

Samuel had a naturally occurring CC muscle genotype.

A superior gene type firmly patented and protected by Myriadsanto.

Myriadsanto responded to this assault upon their Intellectual Property (IP) by sending multiple cease-and-desist letters—but to no avail. Samuel kept growing. It is estimated that "Pirate" Samuel created more illegal copies of Myriadsanto's patented gene in a day than all the Swedish BioHack factories pirated in a week. Left without any other choice, one year after Pirate Samuel's birth, the corporation filed its first lawsuit.

At that time, the spokesperson for Myriadsanto set out their case, "IP is protected by law, and if infringed upon or otherwise abused, the infringers can be prosecuted. We don't undertake this lightly, but patents are the lifeblood and innovation of our company and this great country. They create jobs, and stealing from us robs everyone."

The only response by the Tree family came from the Samuel's father, Jonas, who replied, "Could you patent the sun?"

This provoked a curt reply from EverGreen Solar: "Yes."

Samuel was blatant in his self-incrimination. Multiple recordings show him clapping joyfully while descending slides and giggling while pumping his legs on swings—all the while smiling maliciously. With fines and lawsuits mounting, his parents withdrew him from all physical activity, even breaking their Amish beliefs to provide him with a mobility iChair.

Still, Myriadsanto made it clear: as long as Samuel breathed and his heart pumped, muscles were employed—muscles created by illegally pirated genes.

As a last ditch attempt to avoid justice, the family placed Samuel in a medically induced coma on his third birthday, including an artificial heart and lungs. However, Myriadsanto legal counsel reasonably proved that, despite atrophy, muscle production was still taking place. Moreover, based on the number of reproduced copies of the CC muscle genotype, Myriadsanto showed that Samuel Tree owed fines of more than six quadrillion Amazon Dollars—eight times the world's money supply.

As a result of this unprecedented illegal and high volume piracy, and since the Tree family had made no substantial efforts to redress their criminal activities, Myriadsanto used an injunction to take ownership of what was legally theirs. At 14:26 today, Myriadsanto Corporation took possession of Samuel Tree at New Brighton Hospital and used GeneBleach™ to purge the CC muscle genotype from "Pirate" Samuel.

Pirate Samuel Tree was subsequently declared clinically dead on June 14, 2064 at 14:34, thus ending his lifelong crime spree.

About the Author:

Michael Donoghue mostly lives in his head, but resides in Vancouver. His stories have appeared in anthologies, literary journals, sci-fi magazines and online. Michael works in healthcare, where he spends much of his time preoccupied with hand washing. You can follow him on twitter @mpdonoghue.

De-Sell

by J. Scott Marlatt

Like every other time I'd been there, incense hung in the air so thick I could taste it. Like every other time, I didn't want to know what it was covering up.

Oria trailed a dark, slender finger along her disgusting albino snake while she considered my request. The thought of touching the damned white and pale-orange monstrosity made me gag. It wasn't the creepiest thing in that rickety little shack, either. I knew she was some kind of shaman priestess or whatever, but really, did she have to embrace *every* stereotype?

"Oh me Benny . . ." She trailed that same finger over my forearm then tapped the end of my nose with it. "Jus' why do I be wantin' ta do dat now?"

I brushed the caress off my arm before the chills took over. "You owe me, dearie."

That dimple of hers formed in the smooth chocolate skin of her cheek. Candlelight flickered in the deep wells of her eyes. "Dat debt been paid, Benny. You tellin' me you don recall dat night?"

"That? Kismet, dearie, not payment." That night certainly would have paid the bill, though. Even though I had saved her skin. "Since when did you become a lady of the night?"

Oria's eyes narrowed. Nothing good ever came from that look. "What kinda damn pirate lose 'is map anyway?"

I just stared at her; I wasn't going through that again. After a few moments I gave her *my* winning smile.

"Oh, fine, Benny. I'll ask da Lady if she know anyting." She took a tin off a shelf that looked like it was clinging to the wall by a splinter.

"I'll just wait outside." That damned voodoo crap never sat right in my gut.

"No, no. You stay rite dere, Benny. Da Lady tinks you pretty as I do." She reached in the tin. "Beside, you won be rememberin' dis anyways."

With a flick of her wrist, powder flashed in the air before me and the world went fuzzy.

Sometime later the world began to congeal back around me. Oria dabbed a cloth at the corner of my mouth. Parts of me were . . . numb.

"Did you have to put me to sleep with that powder?"

"Da powda?" Oria tapped the end of my nose. "Hah! Da powda jus' call da Lady, Benny. Ya sleep coz ya can' wrap ya mind 'round her."

"Well, does she have a quicker way for me to find what I seek? Besides digging up the whole damned island?" A lumpy cloth covering several items on the table before me indicated she did.

"A'course, Benny. Dis de Lady we talkin 'bout—"

Something slithered past my leg. I jumped up into the chair, clutched the edge of the table.

Oria laughed. "Ya always been a chicken shit, Benny. Yer boys know dat bout you?"

I glared at her. "They know I'm not fond of snakes, dearie."

"Snakes? Da snake be o'er in dat corna." She pointed to the far side of the room.

I didn't ask. I just slid down Indian style into the chair. If something brushed my legs there, two feet off the ground, I was out of that cursed shack, lost treasure be damned.

Oria laughed again. "Oh, Benny." She shook her head. "Da Lady know wat ya need an' where ta get it. Dere be a man on a isle no far from 'ere—an Englishman—he got wat ya need. Ya be needin' tree tings. Dis—" She whipped back the edge of the cloth. "Dis be getting ya dere."

She picked up a silver amulet on a thin silver chain. The amulet was a perfect circle. Besides some jagged lines and a tiny star etched on the surface, it was unremarkable. She handed it to me.

"How will this get me there?"

She scoffed. "Ow da 'ell should I know?"

"How the hell—really?"

She looked at me like I'd asked her why God put us here. No help there, obviously. "Sorry, dearie. Please go on."

She whipped the cloth back a bit further, revealing a dingy old corset. "Dis be gettin' him ta help ya."

"A corset?"

"Ya."

I felt like I was stating the obvious at that point. "And what am I supposed to do with that?"

"Wear it."

"Is it a *magic* corset?"

She thought it over. "Yah, les go wi' dat."

My hands flopped down to my sides. "Look, you want to consider that beautiful night we had payment of your debt . . . there's really no need to screw with me."

"Ya wan' da Lady's help or no?"

"Just as long as it's actually 'help' this time around, not another fiasco like I got three years ago."

"Oh, Benny. Ya got ezactly wat ya asked for las' time." She shook a finger at me. "Ya has ta be specific wit da Lady, ya know."

I leaned forward. "I want something to help recover what was taken from me."

"Well, dats wat I be askin her for ya."

I considered her for a moment then swept my hand before me to say 'please continue.'

She pulled the cloth all the way back and tossed it aside. She picked up the smaller square of dingy cloth it had been covering. "Dis be da final ting ya need. Ask da man; he be knowin' wat dis be." She handed it to me. "Ya jus' be sure an' bring dis ting. Knowin' ya, ye be forgettin'."

There was a sketch on the cloth. A simple cylinder with a smaller cylinder on top—like a castle rook with a look-out building on top, although the top edge was smooth, not crenellated.

"What the—Wait, I know: 'Ask da man'"

She gave me a grin that made me wish I could get her back in my debt, considering how she preferred to pay off such things.

* * * * *

A week later, I stepped back aboard *The Dirty Knave*, glad to have that stinking swamp far behind me. The enchanting green-blue of Caribbean shallows stretched out to port; the purer blue of deeper waters reached out to starboard until it met the horizon.

Ignacio, my first mate, greeted me. "Welcome back, Captain Cooke." A grizzled old seadog, he'd been sailing long before I was an itching in some soldier's pants. The hair of his scraggly beard was well on its way from peppered to full-on gray. Scars from too many battles to count scattered across olive-oil skin. One in particular—a thick, faded scar across his left cheek—had been the only reminder he'd ever needed about who was captain of *The Knave*. His chins jiggled while he talked—we both needed to get back to raiding, spend less time lounging about while the boys dug holes. Unfortunately, I didn't much care for pillaging. It was much too involved. And messy.

"How was Oria, that ol' witch? Did ya stoke up her furnace again?" Ignacio spoke rather loudly.

"No, it wasn't that kind of trip."

He gave me a cross-eyed look, indicating the deck around me. Several of the men had stopped in their work, eavesdropping.

"Oh, right," I said under my breath. I continued in a boisterous voice: "I'm kidding. Of course I did; I plowed her like . . . like a dirty field." I scrunched my nose at Ignacio.

The boys cheered me and got back to work. Ignacio nodded:

'good enough.'

He noticed the amulet hanging from my neck amongst my usual gold chains. "That's new."

I took off my tricorne and pulled the chain over my head. "Yeah, she gave it to me. Said it'd get us where we needed to go." I'd been studying the damn thing the whole week, and nothing. "I got no idea how it's supposed to do that."

Ignacio took the amulet from me, spun it on its chain. He pinched the bottom between thumb and finger and flicked the edge with his other thumb.

The amulet flipped open on a hidden hinge in the edge opposite Ignacio's thumb.

I snatched it from him. "How the hell—"

By the look on his face, he didn't have a clue.

Folded open all the way, the two long edges—what had been the diameter of the amulet—did not quite make a flat line. The metal came apart in a way that formed a very distinctive pattern of peaks and valleys. I'd seen that horizon before.

I bellowed for my third. "Cesar!"

A massive hunk of tanned, muscly bumps came lumbering up from below decks. A crop of sun-bleached hair sat atop a stern face. Cesar was my master-at-arms. "Uhh?" he grunted.

"Leave four men, men you can trust—well, as far as one can trust a pirate . . . . Anyway, pick four men to guard the island. We're leaving."

"Uhn." That was an affirmative grunt. Cesar turned and started barking out names down the hole he'd come up from.

"Ignacio." I turned back to my first mate. "We sail for the Egret Isles."

* * * * *

From the bow of *The Dirty Knave*, I held up the amulet, open against the oncoming horizon. When I lowered the amulet, the peaks of the Egret Isles matched the peaks on the amulet exactly. The amulet's one little star lay directly below one of the smaller isles.

I couldn't help but smile.

I spun and sauntered off towards my cabin. I tossed the amulet in the air and caught it in my shirt pocket. As I passed Ignacio at the wheel, I yelled out, "Take us to the little one, two to starboard."

"Aye, aye, Cap'n." Ignacio had a twinkle in his eye to match that in my step.

I shut the door to my cabin and set the latch. None of the boys would be so bold as to spy on me, but there was certainly a chance they'd stumble in without thinking.

Much of the walls were covered with books. Books were the one valuable thing most pirates never thought to steal. Probably because most of them couldn't read—unless the words were on a map. As such, books were the last place a pirate tended to look for other valuable things.

I took the heavy iron key out of my copy of *Simplicissimus* and went over to the big oak chest at the foot of the bed. The hinges and seams were all fitted with iron trim. I knelt and unlocked the chest with the key. I ran my finger through a seam on the chest's side until I found the hidden switch that truly unlocked the thing. I stood and lifted open the heavy lid.

That dirty old corset stared mockingly up at me from atop my other treasures. I stood, fists on hips, shaking my head at the damned thing.

Screw it. I ripped off my shirt and went to work.

Lacing it was a mean chore. When I first started struggling, I caught myself calling out to the boys for help and immediately swallowed the cry with a feeling of idiocy. No way I wanted to go down in history as Bloody Ben, The Dainty Raider.

Every time I got those laces down the back of the thing tight, I lost all the tension trying to get it tied. After nearly hanging myself from the rafters attempting to get gravity to help out some, I finally came up with an idea. I got the laces tied as tight as I could, took my pistol's ramrod, stuck it through the laces under the knot, and twisted until I had trouble breathing. I tucked the end of the rod into the higher laces to keep it in place and hoped to God it didn't come loose and unleash the whirlwind on the top of my ass.

Looking back, I'm not sure why I had it in my head that the thing had to be put on proper. I guess I figured if it had been simply a matter of having the thing on my person, it would have been a magic kerchief or something. A magic corset was a corset for a reason.

I grabbed my least puffy shirt—well, I tried; they're all pretty puffy—and headed back to the deck. The crew was already dropping anchor off of the small isle. The place was a mass of thick jungle ringed with a white-sand beach.

Ignacio saw me coming. "Do you want we should circle around the thing, Captain?"

"No, continue anchoring here."

"Just to scope the place out?"

I glared at him. "The star is here; this is where we go ashore."

"Aye, Captain." He studied me a moment. "You're looking rather svelte today, Captain. Have you lost weight?"

I told him to shove it.

He looked hurt. "It was just a compliment."

I told him *where* he could shove it.

I could feel my guts pressing together; things were moving to places they weren't supposed to be. I wanted to get on that island and get it over with already. "Just go and get the ship's tender ready for the two of us."

"The two of us? No support?"

I gave Ignacio a look that said 'just do it' and tried to keep my guts from spilling out both my ends.

I found Cesar shouting at some deck hand over something. Something trivial most likely.

"Cesar! The first mate and I will be going ashore. Prepare to take over the ship in my absence."

"Uhn."

"Just keep her anchored here and await our return."

"Uhn."

I leaned in to him, lowered my voice. "If they turn on you while I'm away, I'm not sure I'll have trouble understanding."

"I'd like to see them try."

I patted him on the shoulder. "Just take it easy, Cesar. Pirates are pirates because they don't like rules, remember."

I didn't get a grunt this time, but I left it at that and joined Ignacio in the tender.

He sulked all the way to shore, which is hard to do when you're rowing.

* * * * *

We found nothing on the beach, apart from crabs—Ignacio fit in perfectly.

I studied the amulet, traced our angle of approach through the point where the star lay, and continued it out into the island's jungle. I pointed toward my calculated route. "We need to head that way."

"Are you sure to don't want to just circle the isle once?"

"You that afraid of a little exercise? Grab the cutlass."

"The what?"

"God . . . the machete." Sometimes it's impossible to remember where everyone comes from.

Ignacio handed me the machete, and we headed off into the jungle. Not twenty feet in it grew so thick, I had to start hacking.

I couldn't get a good swing going with my guts all scrunched up as they were. I damn near lost my footing with each swing. I should've figured how important waist movement was to sword work. I had a hard time ducking branches too. One particularly stubborn tangle of branches knocked my tricorne off. Instinctively, I tried bending over to pick it up. I don't think I even got lower than my knees. I had to bend at the knees to pick it up with my torso nearly straight.

"You hurt your back or something, Cap'n?"

I stabbed the cutlass into the ground. "You're awfully nosy today, mate."

After staring him down for a few moments, I yanked the cutlass out of the ground and went back to hacking. I heard Ignacio mutter, "And you're awfully grumpy today, *mate*," but I said nothing. I took it out on the undergrowth with an especially nasty swing. Of course, I missed completely, spun around in more than a complete circle and collided with the trunk of a huge tree. I think I felt part of my liver disconnect from somewhere.

Ignacio did a good job of studying the local fauna and pretending not to laugh.

I went back to hacking. Things started to get numb. My nose tingled, then the rest of my face, then my arms. I dropped to my knees, panting.

"Captain?"

It was a moment before I could speak. "I think . . . I think you better take over for a while."

"Aye, Cap'n." As he took the cutlass, his eyebrows raised as if to say 'Guess I'm not the only one that needs some exercise.'

I was too busy trying not to die to respond.

Ignacio swung the cutlass a few times with ease, looked over his shoulder at me, and rolled his eyes.

I stood and took a few steps after him. Just as I was raising my hand to put him in his place with a witty and cutting jibe, the world fuzzed to black.

* * * * *

I woke up on my back, nestled between the buttress roots of a huge kapok tree. Some kind of parrot was squawking to high heaven in the branches above. The pressure was gone from my guts; I could breathe.

Ignacio was fanning me with my tricorne. My shirt was off, wadded up in a ball behind my head. The corset hung loosely around my torso. I swatted at Ignacio's hand, snatched my hat back.

He took it all much better than he had everything to that point. A snarky little smirk curled up the corner of his mouth. "Umm, Captain—"

"Shut up." I stood up and brushed the jungle floor off of me.

Curiosity was going to force me to murder this cat. "Cap'n, what the hell are ya doing with that—"

I threw a finger into Ignacio's face. "Shut. Up." I held my finger there until he conceded.

"Shutting up, sir."

The bugs were eating me up. I threw my shirt back on, but let it hang loose and un-tucked. I pulled the cutlass out of the ground and tried to figure out the direction we'd been heading. After finding our back trail, I hacked on through the jungle's undergrowth. It felt good to be able to move freely again.

Ignacio just couldn't hold it all in. "They make those for men, you know."

I let out a great sigh and turned back to him, dragging a half-circle in the dirt around me with the tip of the cutlass. "They make *magic* corsets for men, do they? Well, why didn't I think of that?"

"Magic corsets . . .? So Oria—"

"Of course Oria gave it to me. Why in the bloody hell do you think I'd wear such a thing?" I pointed the tip of the cutlass at his Adam's apple. "Now, shut up."

"Aye, Cap'n."

I spun on my heels and resumed hacking at the jungle. I swear Ignacio was timing snorts and chuckles with my swings the entire way.

* * * * *

Less than fifty feet further in the undergrowth began to thin. The jungle opened up to reveal a hidden cove, accessible from the opposite side of the island we'd approached. Anchored just off-shore was a ship unlike any I'd ever seen.

It was about forty feet long with a gleaming white hull that was so seamless it looked to have been carved from a single piece. It had a single mast and boon, both of which seemed to be . . . metal? The rigging was almost non-existent, just a few cords here and there—ropes far too thin to withstand any light storm. A Union Jack flapped from a short pole on the boat's aft. *The Englishman!*

Just then, a man came into view from the other side of the ship. He swam a last couple of strokes before standing up and wading up onto the beach. Muscles rippled on him wherever he moved—he was a slimmed down version of Cesar—he even had the sun-bleached hair and the golden tan. He picked up a cloth from the beach and dried himself then put on a loose-fitting, short-sleeve shirt that clung to his chest and flapped behind him in the breeze.

I pulled off my own shirt and turned to Ignacio. "Alright, lace me back up."

He slumped his shoulders at the indignity, but went right to work.

Getting a corset on with two men is not much easier than getting one on alone. I guess experience is everything. It didn't help that Ignacio's fingers are like plump little sausages, or that I felt the unfortunate need to breathe. Every time he started to make headway, I'd gasp for air and he'd lose his grip on the laces.

"Listen," I said, "when we get over there, you be quiet and—"

Ignacio planted a boot on my ass for leverage and heaved. When I felt my liver slide back into that uncomfortable place, I knew he finally had it.

I half whimpered, half groaned under my breath. I gave myself a moment before continuing. "Be quiet and let me do the talking."

"Aye Cap'n."

As I put my shirt back on, I saw that damned smirk curl his lips up again.

* * * * *

We approached along the beach, Ignacio trailing behind me despite my handicap. When the Englishman noticed us, I waved like some merchant, out to hawk my wares.

"You feeling alright, Cap'n?" Ignacio said from behind me.

I turned around, skipped down the beach backwards. "Of course, dearie."

We both stopped dead in our tracks. Heat rose in my cheeks. *Maybe the damned thing is magic after all.*

"Umm . . . I mean, of course I'm alright, you . . . you scurvy dog, you."

Ignacio looked at me like I'd put a knife to his throat then pissed on his boots. We walked on in silence, Ignacio a few steps further behind than before.

The Englishman studied us as we approached, hand over his eyes to block the sun. He seemed pleasantly intrigued at first, then, as he looked around me and saw Ignacio, his lips pressed together, his eyes narrowed, and he looked further down his nose at us.

I stopped in front of him. "Ahoy there, matey." I'm afraid I wasn't as enthusiastic as I should have been; sometimes I loathe the role.

He took another moment to study us, particularly Ignacio, before he spoke. "Good Day, Sir." He extended his hand. "Sebastian Prescott."

I shook his hand. "Captain Benjamin Cooke."

"Captain?"

"Right, you've heard of me then?"

He pursed his lips. "No, can't say that I have."

"Bloody Ben Cooke?"

"No."

"Bane of the Bahamas? The Terror from Tortuga?"

"No, sorry." He wrinkled his forehead. "Did you say Tortuga?"

"Aye." It must be coming back to him.

Ignacio cleared his throat behind me.

"Right." I indicated Ignacio. "This be my first mate, Ignacio."

The Englishman looked down his nose again. "Right. Morning." His face perked up, and he looked to me. "First mate? So, you've a ship somewhere near?"

"Aye. Speaking of ships, that's a mighty fine lady you've got there. I've never seen anything quite like her."

"Really? It's quite a common model."

"Common? Just where arrr you from?"

"Brockenhurst. You? Right." He tapped a finger on my shoulder. "Tortuga."

There was an uncomfortable silence for a few moments. We stood there, nodding at nothing in particular, raising eyebrows and bouncing on our toes, hands in pockets.

"Well, she really is a fine ship, anyway," I said.

"Thank you. I'm afraid she's seen better days, however. We went through quite a nasty storm; bloody near snapped the keel off."

"We?"

"Oh yes, my cabin boy." He called out to the ship. "Sergio. Come down here, lad." He turned back to me, continued his tale. "Came from nowhere, the storm. Nastiest thing I've ever seen— lighting that lit up the entire sky. Thought we'd be swallowed by the sea."

A slender young man had climbed down from the sleek ship's bow and joined us. He had dark olive skin, slick with a sheen of oil. Short, jet-black hair was combed forward on his head, straight up to a point above his brow.

The Englishman put an arm around the lad. "Poor Sergio here was so terrified he couldn't do much more than cling to me like a barnacle." He squeezed the lad, who looked away shyly. "It must've blown us entirely off course, because after the flash, we collided with something in the shallows, and we'd been in the deeps. I see no mention of this isle anywhere on my charts, either."

He looked back at his ship. A tinge of sadness touched his eyes. "She's not fit for sailing with the keel nicked as it is, and I'm afraid we've burnt through all our petrol getting to this cove."

"Petrol?"

His head cocked to the side. "Yes, petrol . . . You're a curious fellow, aren't you?"

I tried to remember I needed something from him.

He ushered Sergio off and the lad skipped off to the ship. The Englishman's eyes followed him as the boy climbed back aboard and disappeared somewhere on the deck.

The Englishman sighed and turned to me. "Ahh, Sergio. He's a good lad. Useless everywhere but below decks, but a good lad, if you catch my meaning." He winked at me.

"I most certainly do not." I did though. I was getting a picture at least.

"Oh, come on. A man with a shirt like that has no idea what I'm talking about?"

"What's wrong with my shirt?"

"Nothing, Ben. I love the frills. And all the jewelry? Come on."

"I'm a pirate."

He grinned. "Oh, sure you are." He went to tap me on the shoulder again, but stopped, suddenly aware of Ignacio's presence again.

Ignacio stood there, a grin splitting his face, his eyes laughing at me. A bead of sweat rolled down his chins.

I sighed as I realized the corset's purpose. "Ignacio, mate. Go on back and have the boys bring the ship around, won't you?"

He was having such a hard time keeping it all in. "Aye aye, Cap'n. You have fun with Mr. Prescott and we'll bring her right around." He wandered back to the path we'd cut in the wood, just a laughing and a sighing.

I'm going to string him from the mast later.

When he was out of earshot, the Englishman chuckled. "He's a jolly old chap. Pity when they let themselves go like that."

"Aye, it is . . ." I swallowed, "dearie."

Quite a long spell of shameless flirting ensued from there, which I would rather not talk about here, thank you very much.

Only once I had the Englishman completely enthralled did I feel comfortable bringing up the reason I was there.

"Well, dearie, I have to admit, I was sent here to find you."

The Englishman looked appropriately confused. "Sent here? Why? Who in the bloody hell knows I'm even here?"

"The type of person that knows things. Trust me, dearie, you don't want to know." I kept on talking before his curiosity broke the spell. "They told me you were the only one that could help me."

"Help you?"

"Find what I'm looking for, of course." I give him a little pat on the end of his nose with a finger.

His eyes perked up. "And what are you looking for?"

"Something lost. Something taken from me and buried on an island not far from here."

"Buried treasure, how exciting."

I stiffened up. I didn't need any more partners in this venture. "Treasure of a sort."

He ran a finger over one of my gold chains. "There's gold in this treasure?" He sensed my hesitation. "Don't worry, darling; the last thing I want to do to your booty is steal it."

Well, that's just what the last guy said.

"So, any gold? Silver? Anything metal?"

What's he getting at? "Aye, there's metal."

The Englishman's face lit up. He slapped the back of my shoulder, kept his hand there and squeezed. "I've got just what you need, then." He called up to the ship. "Sergio. Be a dear and bring the metal detector."

"Metal detector?"

He flashed a smile. "Blimey, I really did end up on the other side of the pond. Well, I don't know what you call 'em here, mate, but you'll see in a sec."

Sergio, apparently permanently oiled, appeared above decks. He carried what I assumed was the 'metal detector'. It was a long metal rod with a box on one end and a metal circle on the other. A wire ran from the circle to the box, twisted around the rod. After climbing down to the beach, Sergio gave the device to the Englishman.

"Ahh, yes. This'll do the trick."

I squinted my eyes at the peculiar thing. "What does it do?"

The Englishman looked at me, baffled. "Really? Well, it detects metal, obviously." He fiddled with some knobs on the box and lifted the circle towards me. When the circle passed over my necklaces, it made a strange whirring sound.

"What kind of devilry is this?" I demanded.

"Do you mean to say you've *never* seen one of these? How odd." He handed the device to me. "Here press this button here, and wave the other end over the ground." He took a handful of strange silver coins out of his pocket. "Now, wave it over my hand."

I did and the thing squealed just as it had over my chains. "Fascinating."

I kept waving the thing over the Englishman's hand, astounded. *Oh, the possibilities!* He stared at me like I was an addle-pate. I didn't care, this 'metal detector' could make me the richest pirate in the Caribbean!

The squeals from the thing grew softer and died out completely. "What has happened; what have I done wrong?"

The Englishman took the device from me and pounded the box with the heel of a fist. "Ahh, it's near out of juice, I'm afraid. That'll be easy enough for you to fix."

I took him at his word, reached for the device. As he handed it back, I remembered the third item, the cloth with the drawing. "Oh!" I took it from my pocket—this must be where it comes in. "You don't happen to know what this is, do you? I was told you'd know."

He glanced at the drawing. "Of course. That's exactly what you'll need, darling. Some d-cells. The thing goes through them like crazy."

I frowned. "What's that? De-sell?"

"Yes, darling. D-cells. Batteries. What you'll need to power the detector." He slid open a hidden compartment on the box and out popped a small, black and gold metal cylinder shaped exactly like the one in the drawing, with the smaller metal cylinder on the end. There was lettering on the side: 'DURACELL'. "Hopefully you don't have to look too hard—they're terribly hard to find now-a-days."

"Now-a-days?"

"Yeah." He was distracted by something offshore. *The Dirty Knave* had just sailed into view at the mouth of the cove, jolly roger unfurled and flapping in the wind over sails and crow's nest. "Ever since 2000 or so, they haven't been using them as much . . ." His voice trailed off.

"Did you say 2000?"

"Yes. Is *that* your ship?"

"As in: the year 2000?"

He turned to me, all the color drained from his face. "Bloody hell, you're really a pirate." He swallowed. "Oh, God, *when* am I?"

His voice faded into the background as I dropped to my knees. What was that she'd said about the *drawing* of the d-cell? Oh, right: "Ya jus' be sure an' bring dis ting. Knowin' ya, ye be forgettin'." Back in her hut in that damned swamp, the witch was laughing at me; her and her Lady had fooled me yet again. I threw my head back and screamed at the heavens.

"Oriiiiaaaaaaaaaa!"

About the Author:

J. Scott Marlatt is an author of speculative fiction, focusing in dark fantasy. Due to an unfortunate and prolonged period of madness, he is also an attorney. Scott currently resides in Columbus, OH with his fiancé and her two cats. He tolerates the cats. Most of the time.

Peg-leg Paige

by Stacy Mills

"Girls can't be pirates," Oliver yells at me as he grabs the sword, hat and treasure map from my hands.

"But . . . but, that's mine." My brother, Oliver, and his friend, Collin, don't hear me. They're already outside, the door slamming behind them as they ignored me.

My plans for the day ruined, I wander around the house. My mom is at the next door neighbor's, my sister is who knows where and my brother and his friend are searching for my hidden treasure.

I was so excited earlier when I found the pirate hat and sword. No one had played with them for ages. They were stuffed at the bottom of the toy box in a corner. Mom even hid buried treasure for me to find and gave me a treasure map. I'm pretty sure the treasure is the last box of Girl Scout cookies. I was looking forward to those Savannah Smiles. Little did I know that Oliver and Collin had a secret wish to play pirates but just couldn't find the props.

Lilypat, my cat, sits on her belly with her chin on her paws, watching me pace. She's sick of being inside too. "Lilypat, we're gonna have fun today," I whisper in her ear. Her tail twitches. She's ready for some fun. I grab her and outside we go.

The sun shines and birds fly around. Lilypat hears a bird chirping and squirms out of my arms. She runs towards her prey, her tail straight up. Running after her brings me to the pond in our neighborhood commons. The pond is a fun place to hang out. We bike around it and swim in it and some people even take small fishing boats in. It's so big that I can't even swim all the way across; I always have to take a break at the wooden platform in the middle that people dive off. We're not supposed to play in the pond though, without Mom or Dad around. That's why when I see what Oliver and Collin are up to, my eyes bug out of my face. They're on a swimming pool raft in the middle of the pond. I'm pretty sure if Mom knew what they were doing, she would be screaming mad. *This has got to be Collin's idea; Oliver would never have the guts to suggest it.*

"Paige, help us. Help us. We're going down!" My brother shouts to me across the pond. I look at him and he's right, he and Collin are going down. It really is his own fault though. Who takes a swimming pool raft into the middle of a pond? I mean, really? I think the problem is that they didn't blow it up enough. As I watch the boys, they sink lower and lower into the water. Their 'pirate ship' is taking on too much water for them to survive much longer.

"Be careful for the sharks," I scream out to them. I giggle.

When I say that, Collin's face falls and he looks like he's going to cry. He sucks in his breath. "Are there really sharks in the pond?"

My giggles turn to full-on laughter. I double over, holding my stomach as my body shakes with howls. I'm only eight and even I know there are no sharks in the middle of a pond in Virginia. Sharks live in the deep ocean. Hasn't he ever seen Shark Week?

"Paige, c'mon, seriously. I'm telling you, we really need help. Get Mom," Oliver says.

I turn and look for my mom. She and our neighbor had been sitting outside on the deck just a little while ago. I guess they decided the weather was too muggy so they went inside.

"Sorry, she's not home right now."

"Paige, do something. I can't swim." Collin has his hands together like in a prayer.

"Fine, paddle with your hands to the platform and I'll figure something out." I turn to my fearless companion, Lilypat. The bird has flown off and Lilypat has joined me watching the show.

"Lilypat, I guess we're gonna get to be pirates today after all."

Lilypat looks me straight in the eye, blinks once, and meows. She agrees. I want to think to myself that this wouldn't have happened if Oliver and Collin had let me play with them earlier, but that is not very nice so I stop thinking it.

"Lilypat, we're going after our treasure. If those scallywags are lucky, we won't make them walk the plank. Are you in?"

Lilypat purrs and does jiggly-tail where she moves her hips back and forth so much that her tail swishes. That's her way of telling me she's up for an adventure.

First things first. If we're gonna be pirates, we have to look the part. "I'll be back soon," I shout to the boys. They've made it to the platform but seem to be in bad spirits. It looks like Oliver took a dip in the pond, he's so wet.

I scoop Lilypat up and carry her into my house. I search through the toy box to see if there are any more pirate accessories. There aren't, but I do see some of my sister, Jemima's, play jewelry. Pirates always wear lots of jewelry so I put on a bunch of necklaces and rings. I run to my room and put on a pair of long shorts and my cowboy boots. The cowboy boots don't quite fit the look I'm going for, but my mom has never bought me any pirate boots.

I find my dad's red bandana and my mom's big, gold, hoop earrings. It's a good thing I got my ears pierced for my birthday. Pirates only wear one hoop earring so I only put one in. I put the bandana over my head like I'm riding a motorcycle. *Good, now I look just like a pirate.*

"Now, what to do with you?" I say to my cat. I snap my fingers. "I know!" I run to the recycle bin and grab some newspaper. It takes me a few minutes but I finally make a tiny pirate hat out of newspaper. I even put holes in it for Lilypat's ears to stick through.

"That's not quite good enough."

Lilypat cocks her head and looks at me with her ears tilted

back a little. That takes a lot of effort for her, you know, because of the pirate hat. I color a piece of gauze black and put two pieces of string through the sides. It's a perfect eye patch for her. I put it over her right eye.

Lilypat takes her paw and ties to rub the eye patch off. "No, no, Lilypat. To be a pirate cat you have to have an eye patch."

Lilypat makes a pitiful mrrw but doesn't take it any further.

I look at myself in the mirror. "Aargh." I say to my reflection, making the scariest pirate face I can.

Lilypat tries her own aargh right after me, only hers sounds like a meow.

"That's okay, Lilypat. Good try. You'll get it next time." I tickle Lilypat's chin, pick her up and run outside.

"PAIGE, where have you been? Come get us, now. We're bored." Oliver stands when he sees me. His voice cracks like he's trying not to cry. I must have been gone for a while because he looks drier. Collin sits Indian style on the platform with his head in his hands and his elbows on his knees.

"Ok, ok, hold your horses. I'll go get help." I don't immediately go get help though. I still haven't figured out how I'm going to rescue them. I need some way to get to the platform in the middle of the pond. But what? The swimming pool raft is obviously a bad idea. I don't need to get stuck on the platform with them. I'd never hear the end of it. A canoe might work, but we don't have one. Daddy has a boat, but it's too big for the pond, plus I'm not allowed to drive it without an adult.

"Paige . . . what's the hold up?"

I jerk out of my thoughts. A light bulb goes on over my head. I know what exactly we can use. We have a paddle boat that works by pedaling just like I'm riding a bike.

"I'll be back in a jiffy," I yell to the boys. "Lilypat, you stay here and guard them for me. I'll be lightning fast."

Lilypat lays down by the side of the pond with her head on her paws, her purrs a rumble so loud, I can hear them. She starts eating grass.

I run to the corner of our backyard. The paddle boat is in a shed back there. I grab at the handle to the shed. I yank. Nothing happens. I yank harder. The door still doesn't open. The final time I try, I yank so hard that when I let go, I stumble backwards and fall on my patoot. I glance around me. My cheeks feel warm and I know there is red creeping up my neck to my cheeks. I pat the bandana on my head and the jewelry around my neck to make sure everything's still in place. *Good, no one saw.*

It's a good thing the shed is where it is because the boys can't see me. Could you imagine the teasing I would get, if they saw that? It doesn't matter that I would save them. My fall would be all over the neighborhood. *There goes my reputation, as my sister would say.*

I look at the shed. There's nothing in the way of the door. It should open. Oliver and Collin got the swimming pool raft out of here earlier, so why doesn't the door open? Unless, wait, maybe the shed door is locked? Just to make sure, I try the shed door one more time. I'm careful this time, though. I don't want to make a fool of myself again. I must be taking a long time because Lilypat wanders over to me. I scoop her up. I need to find the key to the shed door.

"Lilypat, do you think Oliver still has the shed key?" She meows. She's right. Why would Oliver take the key out onto the pond? I search the grass around the shed. Maybe he just dropped it. Since I don't see anything shiny by the shed, I run back to the water.

"Hey, do you have the shed key?"

Oliver looks at me and pats his shorts right where his pocket is. He pulls out the key. He cocks his arm.

"No, don't . . ." I scream. Too late. The key plops in the water. He threw the key before I could finish my sentence. I collapse on the ground. *Now, how am I supposed to save them?* Lilypat walks away but stops and, turning to look at me, meows to get me to follow her. She does this all the way into the house. She stops by the key ring. *Of course, the spare!* In the kitchen, I search the junk drawer, the key ring and Mommy's purse, but I can't find the spare anywhere.

I suppose I need to go find Mom. Since she's not outside any longer, I guess she's in the neighbor's house. As Lilypat and I walk across our yard to the neighbors' yard, I try to put Lilypat on my shoulder so she can be like a parrot. She won't sit up there though. Instead, she climbs around my neck and back into my arms. I knock on the neighbor's backdoor. I hear my mom's laughter somewhere in the house.

"Paige, I bet you're looking for your mom. Well she's right in the living room. Feel free to go inside," Mrs. Fautz says.

"Well ahoy there and shiver me timbers, look at you." Sometimes Mom's so embarrassing. She turns to Mrs. Fautz. "Look at how Paige is dressed, and she put an eye patch on Lilypat. What a creative daughter I have." Mom winks at our neighbor.

My mom's right. I am very creative. But I don't have time for compliments; I have a brother to save. "Mom, where's the spare key to the shed?"

"Oh, honey. I don't know. Can I give it to you later?"

"No, Mom, it's important I get it now."

"Have you looked for it already?" I nod. I tap my foot. Mom sees it and smiles. "Does this have something to do with finding your treasure?" I nod again. "Okay, let me think. Where have you looked already?" I list off all the places I've already looked. "Well, honey, I think the only other place it could be is on the key ring in the pantry."

The pantry, of course! Why didn't I think of that?

"Thanks, Mommy," I say in a sing song voice like I've heard my sister use as I leave the house. Lilypat and I run like we're in a sprint to the house. I grab the key from the pantry and run outside again. Lilypat has not liked the jostling I've given her so as soon as we're outside again, she jumps from my arms and runs beside me to the shed. After unlocking the door, I yank on the doorknob. This time the door swings open.

The paddle boat is propped up against the wall behind the lawnmower and a bike. It's been a while since I've seen the paddle boat and I've forgotten how huge it is. "Oops, Lilypat, we might've bitten off more than we can chew."

I have to move the lawnmower and bike and a bunch of other stuff before I can push the paddle boat over. It's pretty heavy but it's a good thing I have muscles. I switch between pushing and pulling the paddle boat out from the shed and down to the pond. The paddle boat is almost in the water when I realize it's incomplete. You can't have a pirate ship without a flag. How else are people going to know to be scared of us?

I draw a skull and bones on an old t-shirt and I mount my pirate flag to the back of the paddle boat. Now Lilypat and I really are pirates.

I finally get the paddle boat into the water. I see something shiny in the weeds by the pond. It's the pirate sword Oliver took from me. I grab it. I place Lilypat in the seat where she immediately begins washing her feet. I push the paddle boat in as far as I can. It starts to drift away. "Shoot, Lilypat, stay put."

She's not concerned though. Now she's washing her stomach. But when she hears her name, she looks up at me and seems to realize that she's on a boat. She barely opens her mouth when she meows. Each meow is just a syllable. Sometimes her mouth opens but no sound comes out. She's not happy to be a pirate now. I'm having trouble consoling her though because the boat is drifting away from me. The wind has definitely picked up since we were outside before. If I don't get onto the boat soon, it will glide too far away. *Wouldn't I be a hero if I had to rescue Lilypat and the boys?*

I splash into the shallow end of the pond. The boat is moving so fast I have to run after it. With each step, water splashes up at me. Water gets into my boot. They are getting heavier and heavier and are sinking into the mud.

Lilypat's meows are much louder now. She stands on the seat, probably trying to decide if she should make a break for it.

Throughout all of this, Oliver and Collin have been surprisingly silent. I look over at the platform. The boys aren't even watching so that explains why they aren't making fun of me. Instead, they are looking over me at the sky. I turn around too. The clouds behind me are dark, almost black. A storm is definitely rolling in.

I grab the back of the boat and climb in. I take a few moments to pet Lilypat and she calms down. She doesn't lay down, but she does sit without crying. I pedal but the boat still drifts. I pedal harder.

This whole pedaling thing is a lot tougher than it looks. I guess when Daddy and I go out on the pond, he does most of the work, and here I was thinking I was super strong. I consider putting Lilypat down on the pedals and telling her what to do, just so I can get some help pedaling. But, her paws are too short.

She seems to have gotten over her sea-sickness. She's on the bow of the pedal boat with her front paws on the metal. She turns her head and I can see a smile on her face. She is doing king of the world just like in Mommy's favorite movie, *Titanic*. She's even purring so much that I can hear it over the rush of the wind and the water lapping against the boat.

"C'mon Paige, c'mon, you're almost here. Hurry up. Keep going." The encouragement I'm getting from Oliver and Collin is nice. Of course, it's totally to benefit them since they want off that platform so much they can taste it.

The dark clouds are just over us when I reach the platform. My hair whips around.

"Good, you're here. Move, I want to get on." Oliver says. I stand in his way so he can't get onto the boat.

"No, you're gonna have to give me my treasure to get on this pirate ship. I want ye treasure." I say.

"Treasure, what treasure?" Oliver says.

I point the sword at his belly, "The treasure ye stole from the great pirate, Peg-leg Paige." The boys argue with me but in true pirate fashion, I won't let them get on the boat without my treasure. I even threaten to make them walk the plank.

A big raindrop lands on Oliver's arm. Then another and another "Fine, here you go." Just in time, Oliver thrusts the treasure bag at me. I step aside and let the boys scramble onto the paddle boat. They put the canopy up so we don't get rained on. I sit down in the back with Lilypat and open the treasure bag.

"Oh look, Lilypat, Mom put cat treats in the bag for you too." While Oliver and Collin pump their legs like their lives depend on it, Lilypat and I sit back, eat our treats and watch the rain hit the water. With the wind blowing waves into the pond, I almost imagine Lilypat and myself aboard a real pirate ship.

And that's how I showed my brother girls can be pirates.

About the Author:

Stacy Mills writes speculative fiction for middle grade and young adult readers. A self-proclaimed expert in all things feline, she firmly believes that the world would be a better place if it had more cats. Stacy graduated from Denison University, an excellent school that could, of course, use more cats.

Mutiny

by Andrew Knighton

The Atlantic wind snapped at Captain Bradey, his hands half-frozen on the wheel. That fierce easterly had led the Isabella to two fat Spanish merchant ships in the past month, but he still cursed its cold and wished for a thicker coat. Riches warmed his heart, but his body felt like ice.

A cry went up from the foredeck, the bosun's voice high with a panic that infected Bradey. Were the navy onto them again? They'd barely got away with their lives last time, and the Isabella had been fighting fit then.

He handed the wheel to Sands and rushed off down the deck.

Half the crew stood muttering anxiously at the prow, eyes fixed on the figurehead, which had been turned to face back up the ship. Paint peeled from the wooden woman and woodworm pocked her cheeks.

"What's got you lubbers in such a stir?" Bradey asked.

The figurehead raised her arm

He stood stunned. In all his years, he'd never seen anything so uncanny as this figure blinking her flaking eyes.

"You," she rasped, through lips once cherry red. "Turn us south."

Bradey took a deep breath. He'd seen things nearly as strange. That hairy-tailed Frenchman at Gateshead, or the striped horses in Benin. He could cope with this.

"I ain't changing course," he said, trying not to tremble as he wondered what dark spirit had animated this thing. "This here is the tip of the Golden Triangle. We're making a fortune."

"I am old and tired." The figurehead frowned, paint cracking on her forehead. "I want warmth and sunshine. Turn us south."

"Not happening," Bradey said, his courage growing. "We've taken a lot of risks for our fortunes. We ain't wasting that so some wood can retire."

"It's not just me. The sails agree."

With a whirring of ropes, the sails flapped free. As she lost the wind, the Isabella slowed, while more of the crew gathered round. Pirates were a superstitious bunch, and they clutched their crosses at the uncanny sight. But they were a mutinous bunch too, fast to criticize and faster to attack. If they thought this was Bradey's doing, or that he was losing control, then they'd turn on him.

Bradey battled down his growing anxiety. Something was itching at his brain. He smelt a scam.

"If you can do that, why not just sail south?" he asked.

"The tiller," the figurehead said scornfully. "Too much time being pawed by human hands. It's on your side."

Bradey glanced round at his crew. He couldn't look soft. They were already muttering among themselves, toying with their cutlasses.

"This is mutiny," he declared. "I won't stand for it."

"And I won't stand for another day of frost on my paintwork."

The wind was growing, tongues of icy rain lashing at Bradey's face. He thought about fetching the cat-o-nine-tails, but what use would that be on a lump of wood. Panic mounting, he grabbed a lantern from its hook.

"Set the sails, or I'll set you on fire," he said. Oil sloshed around the lamp as the ship tilted.

"Will you burn the sails as well?" the figurehead asked. "And the rigging, the trapdoors, the gun ports?"

Doors slammed like thunderclaps, the whole ship echoing her words.

"Maybe they'll learn from your charred example," Bradey said.

"And maybe you'll burn down the ship," said the figurehead.

"Can you captain flames?"

The wind was howling now, threatening to hurl Bradey into the sea. Men swayed spider-like in the rigging, trying to haul in the sails, but the canvass ripped itself from their hands. Others still stood watching him, and a spokesman was stepping forwards, a cutlass in his hand. Someone younger and stronger than Bradey. Someone who thought he could do this better.

Bradey grabbed an axe from its mounting. One hand clutching the rail, he waved the blade in the figurehead's face.

"This I can control," he yelled, his words snatched away on the storm. "End your mutiny, or I'll turn your pretty face to kindling."

"I'm the only part of the ship with ears," she said. "The only one with a mouth. Smash me, and you can't talk with the rest. They'll writhe and fight as the storm sinks us. But better that than this endless cold."

Bradey staggered as a wave crashed against the bow. His feet slid across wet boards, numb fingers barely clinging onto the axe. And through the spray, the challenger strode towards him, black spot in his outstretched hand.

He stared defeat in the face. He was soaked and frozen and miserable. He couldn't govern his ship, couldn't govern his crew, and if he was lucky he might get demoted to bilge cleaning instead of murdered. Some fights you couldn't win.

Others maybe you shouldn't.

"Fine," he said. "You win."

He swung the axe, hacking the legs out from beneath his startled challenger. Blood sprayed across the deck.

The crew gawped, caught between failure and their next plan.

Bradey seized the moment.

"Mister Sands, set a course south," he bellowed. "I've had enough of this god-awful weather."

The crew turned uncertainly to each other.

"Sunshine, dusky maidens, and all the rum you can drink,"

Bradey called out. "What d'you say lads?"

With a chorus of approval, they returned to their stations. The air of mutiny had dispersed, for now.

Bradey smiled at the figurehead.

"You win," he said.

"Don't we all?" she replied, and turned to face south.

About the Author:

Andrew lives in Stockport, England, where the grey skies provide a good motive to stay inside at the word processor. He's had over forty stories published in places including Wily Writers, Redstone SF and the Ann VanderMeer's Steampunk anthologies. You can find out more at andrewknighton.wordpress.com .

Rings and Waves

by Shenoa Carroll-Bradd

A strange pair of travelers stopped on the wharf before the sailing vessel *The Uncrowned Queen*. The woman wore a high silver collar from chin to shoulder, and her male companion regarded the ship with a pale face so smooth it might have been a mask.

"I don't like this," the woman said.

"Nor do I, my lady, but it is the fastest way back to the halls of my creators. Traveling by wagon would add an extra two weeks to our journey."

She shifted her grip on the luggage. "So? You haven't seen that place in decades. What does another fortnight matter?"

The man turned to her and cocked his head. "This conversation would have been more useful three days ago. We are here now, a stone's throw from boarding. We are going."

She sighed, and her shoulders slumped beneath the collar. "Sea travel didn't sound so bad before, but now that we're here, looking at it . . . and the ocean . . . ." She gripped the luggage with both black-gloved hands. "I've never been on a boat before."

"Nor have I, my lady. It will be quite an adventure." He started forward onto the gangplank.

"No, wait!" She grabbed his arm and pulled him back a few steps. "Gus, I can't . . . swim."

He raised an eyebrow, creating neither wrinkle nor crease on his smooth complexion. He rapped two knuckles against his chest, making a heavy, solid echo. "Do you suppose I can?" He took her hand off his arm and entwined his fingers in her own, their gloves contrasting, white on black. "Cheer up," he told her. "I'll be with you the whole way."

"And if we sink?"

"As I said, my lady. The whole way."

When they reached the main deck the ship's porter, a young man with freckles and a chipped front tooth, stepped out from behind a makeshift podium to greet them.

"Hallo, and welcome aboard *The Uncrowned Queen.* Is your name already on the ship's roster, or will you need to arrange a booking today?"

"We spoke with Captain Briggs yesterday," the woman supplied. "We should be on your roster. Elisandre Mirot, and—"

"Vrai," Gus corrected.

She paused for a moment then slowly nodded. "Yes, that's correct. I have yet to adjust to that. Elisandre Vrai. Elise, if you please."

The porter made a little note in his ledger. "Very good. Lady Vrai, and . . ."

"Guissard," she said. "No surname, just . . . Guissard."

The pale man looked as if he might have something to say on that point, but ultimately decided to keep it to himself.

"All sorted, then." The porter made one more mark in his book then set the quill down. "If you'd just follow me, I'll show you to your cabin."

Their quarters were cramped, as was to be expected. A bed took up half the space, with a perfunctory window on the back wall and a small shelf bolted into the wall. The porter stacked their luggage beside the bed, maintaining a respectful demeanor, but still stealing furtive glances at Guissard, and at Elise's silver collar.

When she noticed, Elise touched two fingers to the metal. "I'm recovering from an injury."

The porter nodded and smiled, but his curiosity seemed far from quenched. He seemed to take in all of their luggage and belongings with a touch too much interest, but at last, he left them to unpack. "There'll be a gathering on deck in about an hour," he said. "The captain likes to say a short hello before setting sail."

"Been in his service long?" Gus asked, opening a bag and

unpacking his jeweler's tools, watchmaker's supplies, and a half-finished music box.

The boy's eyes went wide. "Yes sir, stuck with him through good times and lean."

Gus turned to his project, and the porter watched with sparkling eyes.

Elise frowned. "Anything else?"

"Oh, no my lady. That's all for now." He bowed and left.

Elise closed the door behind him. "He was an odd fellow."

"No. He was normal. We're the odd ones." Gus looked up from his project. "You must get used to being a curiosity, my lady."

She sank onto the bed with a sigh, kneeling on the blankets to peer out the window. The view was only a vague impression of light and dark, blurry shapes wheeling in the sky, and the great expanse of the dark ocean, spreading out forever. She shivered. "There's far too much ocean out there. It's not decent."

Guissard set down his tools. "You need to put it out of your mind. It's just water."

"How can I? We're about to be surrounded by it."

"Hush now," he chided sweetly. "Find some way to distract yourself. Would you like to wind me?"

"Do you need to be wound?"

"I will by the time we meet the captain. Better early than late." He sat at the edge of the bed, facing away from her, elbows moving as he untied his jabot. He pulled a fine chain over his head, gathered it in his palm and held it out without looking back.

Elise took the chain and embraced his back, looping her left arm across his chest and resting her chin on his shoulder as best she could with the collar. She gripped the key at the end of the chain and leaned forward to insert it into the keyhole set in the hollow of his throat. She pressed her cheek against his as she turned the key, winding up her automaton. After two turns, she paused. "You can't float, can you?"

"Elise—"

"No, I'm not talking about the ocean anymore. You can't swim and you can't float . . . but you lowered yourself into the well when I fell in, back at the chateau."

"Yes."

"But if the rope had broken, or you had slipped, you would have sunk straight to the bottom. You would have been trapped down there."

His hand closed over hers, gently.

She resumed turning the key.

"A necessary risk. You know I hold your welfare paramount to my own."

Elise continued her task, holding him close. When he was fully wound, two simultaneous clicks occurred within him, one in his head, one in his chest. "There you are."

"Thank you. Wasn't that calming?"

"Yes. You were right." She handed the key back.

Guissard accepted the chain, looped it over his head once more, then took her hand in his. "Elise." He turned on the bed then moved backward, dropping to one knee on the cabin floor.

Her brow furrowed. "What are you doing?"

The automaton held her hand in his, gazing up with green glass eyes, his porcelain face placid. "Would you consider, someday, marrying me?"

She blinked slowly, but did not take her hand away. "Gus . . ."

He looked down and released her hand. "I should not have gotten on my knees. I see that now. It was a miscalculation." He rose and retook his seat beside her on the bed. "I'm not asking for an answer now. Just, someday. Think on it."

She brushed the hard plane of his cheek with the back of her hand. "Someday, perhaps. Unless we find that your creators built a mate for you—"

"I don't care if they did. I've told you—"

"Yes."

"Yes?"

"Someday. Yes." Her hand swept in an arc from his face to

the tall silver collar at her throat. "It's not as if anyone else would have me."

The automaton's shoulders slumped and he turned his face away.

"Oh, no, Guissard, I didn't mean it like that. I'm pleased you asked, really I am."

"It's fine, my lady. I understand." He rose and went to work on his half-finished project.

Elise felt a twinge of guilt, but could think of nothing else to say, so she bent to the task of unpacking.

* * * * *

A brass bell rang out across the ship to call everyone together for the casting-off gathering. Elise and Gus emerged arm in arm from their cabin, close but not speaking. The period between the proposal and the gathering passed almost entirely in silence.

The deck filled quickly with well-dressed passengers, populous, but not too crowded.

Elise glanced around. "Have you noticed the state of the other passengers?"

Guissard looked around as well. "They seem fine to me."

"Yes, they're fine, but they're also all well-off. Not a poor man among them."

Gus scanned the deck once more then shrugged. "Probably common on sailing ships. I have no basis of reference." He touched his lips to her temple. "Stop worrying about everything. Enjoy the adventure."

Captain Briggs stepped out of his quarters and approached the railing with a smile, his crew ranging out behind him. "Welcome aboard *The Uncrowned Queen!*" he bellowed. "Ours will be a brief journey, five days from port to port, so please relax and enjoy the trip." He waved to the men behind him. "If you need anything, my crew is here for you. Please do not hesitate to ask. We'll be getting underway shortly, and dinner will be served at sundown." He gave the assembled passengers a cheerful salute, then began calling out orders to his men.

The passengers exchanged brief introductions before hurrying back to their rooms so as not to block the busy sailors.

The ship lurched and swayed as it set sail. Down in their cabin, Guissard bent over his gadget while Elise lay on the bed with a pillow over her face.

"This is miserable," she mumbled through the fabric. "Will it be this way the whole trip?"

"Your guess is as good as mine." Gus continued his work, occasionally shooting a hand out to catch a rolling tool or escaping cog.

"This lurching is making me wish I could vomit." She moaned.

* * * * *

When the dinner bell chimed, the pair discussed venturing out and socializing with the other passengers, but ultimately decided against it. Instead, they had the porter bring them a tray of food from the galley, for appearance's sake. Once he was gone, they tucked the tray underneath their bed and resumed what they were doing.

* * * * *

The sailing smoothed out after a day, and they emerged to take leisurely walks around the deck, admiring the shining sea from a safe distance.

Captain Briggs hailed them on one of their mid-afternoon passes. "Hello again, you two. Could I have a word? My porter tells me you have yet to take a meal with the other passengers. Anything the matter?"

Elise touched Guissard's arm. "No, thank you. The service has been beyond reproach, but . . . ours is an unusual story. If you find a spare hour for it some night . . . ."

Captain Briggs smiled and touched a finger to his hat. "I do love an interesting story. You are welcome to take a brandy with me tomorrow night, if you like."

"Oh, how wonderful." Elise squeezed her companion's arm and smiled. "We'd love to join you, wouldn't we?"

Guissard nodded. "Naturally. We'd be honored."

When they finished their walk and returned to their cabin, the pair was surprised to find the young porter crouching beside their luggage.

"Why are you in here?" Elise demanded. "What are you doing?"

The porter jumped and turned to face them, his arms stacked with the trays they'd hidden under the bed.

"Cook was wanting these," he said shyly.

"Oh. Sorry. Thank you." Elise did not blush, but she averted her eyes and stepped to the side so he could exit the cabin.

"No need to be so suspicious," Gus murmured.

Elise said nothing else, but she closed up their luggage, biting her lip and trying to remember if they had left the satchels open.

* * * * *

The following night, just after dinner, Captain Briggs welcomed them warmly into his cabin, every inch of which was filled with maps and books. The captain's cheeks were flushed already. Elise suspected he had started enjoying the brandy without them.

Both Elise and Guissard declined his offer of brandy, but they happily seated themselves in his leather chairs.

"Not a drop for either of you? It's a pity. This is a really top-notch bottle. The crew gave it to me this evening, as a bit of a peace offering." The captain settled behind his cluttered desk and refilled his glass. "But enough of that, you didn't come here to hear me prattle. Time for your unusual story I think, if you please."

Elise and Guissard exchanged glances.

"Well, Guissard here is a sophisticated automaton," Elise began, reaching up to untie his jabot to show the captain his keyhole.

The captain's eyebrows shot up.

"He's my companion and protector, and . . . occasionally, physician." She touched the collar. "He's served my family for several generations, as I've just recently learned. It's been an . . . exhausting year."

"We're traveling to the land of my creators," Gus explained. "I want to learn if there were others made like me, and to seek out the truth of my own history."

Captain Briggs whistled and took a sip of brandy. "That is an incredible story indeed. Mine sounds rather shoddy by comparison." He leaned forward, arms braced on the desk. "I've been the captain of this vessel for eight years now, and the crew has been with me for almost all of it." He sipped again. "I've always tried to be fair to the men, but I will admit, the crew hasn't always landed on the right side of the law. I've done a good job of turning their opinions and moral compasses, but . . . some grumblings have resurfaced. I'm sure that if we can carry on with nice, respectable voyages, there will be no more talk of *piracy*." Captain Briggs' eyes went wide, and he leaned back in his chair. "Oh dear. This brandy seems to have loosened my tongue more than usual. I trust you'll keep my confidence?"

"Of course." Elise smiled. "As long as you keep ours. Most people are, understandably, put off by our . . . ." She looked to Guissard, searching for the proper word.

"Peculiarities," he supplied.

"I don't mean to worry you," Captain Briggs continued. "My men seem to have reformed of their own accord. They fully supported this voyage, and I've not heard a cross word about profits or plunder."

"Well." Elise tried on a smile. "That's good to hear, isn't it?"

Guissard nodded. "Yes." He shifted forward in his chair. "I don't mean to impose upon your hospitality, captain, but as long as we're here . . . ." He took Elise's hand and covered it with his own, light over dark. "We've been discussing marriage, and I understand a ship's captain has that power?"

"What?" Elise pulled her hand away. "What happened to some day?"

The automaton turned to her. "Your worries about the well and the sea impressed upon me how quickly fates may change. I see no reason to put off our union any longer." He paused. "Unless you have one."

"I'm not saying no, but shouldn't we wait until we land? So we can have a proper ceremony?"

"Who would we invite?" Guissard asked softly. "And where would we hold it?"

Elise's shoulders slipped lower. "You're right, of course. I just, never pictured my wedding happening in a captain's cabin, while I'm wearing traveling clothes. But then," she touched two fingers to her collar, then she stroked Guissard's pale cheek, "quite a lot has turned out different than I imagined."

"Do you have a ring?" Captain Briggs interjected.

"No," Elise said, "we weren't properly prepared for—"

Guissard reached into a pocket sewn to the inner lining of his vest. "I do."

"Guis, you miracle! When did you find time to purchase a ring? I've been at your side every minute."

He inclined his head and gestured to the captain. "That's a story for later."

Captain Briggs came out from behind his desk and motioned for them to rise. He straightened his coat and removed his hat. "Very well. Mr. Guissard, please repeat after me: With this ring, I thee wed."

Guissard took his bride's gloved hand in his.

She watched each movement with glittering eyes.

"With this ring, I thee—"

Elise's face suffered an immediate transformation as she got a closer look at the ring. She withdrew her hand so fast, the ring fell to the cabin floor with a quiet clink.

Guissard dropped to hands and knees, searching the cabin floor.

"Lady Vrai!" The Captain chided.

"Not with that ring," she said fiercely. "How did you . . . why do you even have that? I threw it away months ago."

Gus looked up from the floor, holding the article in question between thumb and forefinger. "And I retrieved it."

"Clearly," her voice began to shake, "I didn't want you to retrieve it. That's why I threw it away."

He remained on his knees, offering the ring. "In the stories, it's always a test. Fetching the ring. The princess or shepherdess, or—"

"Blast your stories!" Elise hissed. "Enough of this. I won't marry anyone with that ring, not even you." With that, she swept out of the captain's quarters, storming out onto the deck, fists bunched at her sides, eyes down, teeth clenched. The ship rocked and sea spray flew into her eyes. Elise gripped the railing and leaned over, screaming her fury into the throat of the sea. She hit the railing twice, then took a deep breath and walked stiffly to her room.

* * * * *

The captain placed his hat back on his head. "What was that about?"

Guissard looked down at the ring in his gloved palm. "It was her mother's." He closed his fingers around the ring and tucked it back into his vest pocket. "I feared she might react this way."

"Not a happy relationship then?"

Guissard gave him a funny half-smile. "No. Nor with her father, the poor thing. But I thought ahead, and I have a replacement ring on hand. Grant me just a moment, and I'll have her back."

"Best of luck to you," Captain Briggs said. "Hurry though, my head is getting heavy. This brandy seems to be doing a number on me."

Gus nodded and stepped out onto the rocking ship deck. Elise was nowhere in sight. He headed toward their cabin, but as he crossed the deck, several figures approached from either side. Crewmembers, sailors he'd seen often enough before, but now they wore dark clothes and seemed to be armed. Guissard walked faster.

"Your woman was in an awful brew," one called from the left.

Gus narrowed his eyes. "She's not my woman." His hand came up to press against the hidden ring. *Not yet at least.*

"Is it because she hasn't got a real man?" another jeered. "You can't keep her too warm at night, can you?" The men moved together to form a leering, ill-humored wall between him and his quarters.

Guissard's hands curled into steely fists. "She does not complain. Now, if you'll please . . . ." He pushed through them, intent on reaching the cabin where Elise waited.

"No, she wouldn't complain, would she?" One of them scoffed. "Whores never do."

Guissard spun on his heel and grabbed the nearest man with his extendable steel arms.

* * * * *

Inside the cabin, Elise sat on their bed, knees drawn up, head in her hands. How could he? Gus understood her complicated past better than anyone. He should have known the sight of that ring would upset her.

An envelope on the shelf that Gus had turned into his temporary workbench caught her eye. Her name was written across its face in his careful, precise hand. She rose and opened it.

The note inside read:

Elise,

If you're reading this, then I've made a mistake, and you are probably annoyed with me. Apologies for that.

She sniffled and looked into the envelope. Something weighted the bottom. She dumped it out onto her palm before reading the rest.

I brought your mother's ring because I hoped you could learn to reconcile your past with our present. If you are not ready yet, I understand and support you fully. But we cannot walk away from our heritage, no matter how hard we try. It is a deep and irrevocable part of us all.

Until the day you are ready to face that, please wear this ring instead. As you've seen, I do not have a heart to offer, but this ring is a duplicate of a cog that occupies a similar space in my chest. I would be honored if you wore it.

~ Gus

Elise stared at the cog in her hand. It was steel, not gold or silver, like most wedding bands, and all the teeth except those at the very top had been filed away, so that when she slipped it onto her finger, the remaining teeth stood proud like the rays of the sun, or a fairy crown. It fit her perfectly.

The cabin door opened.

"Oh Gus, I'm sorry for being cross." She sat the envelope and note back on the shelf before turning. "Thank you for being so patient with—" Her eyes went wide as she faced the men blocking the doorway. "What do you think you're doing, entering without invitation? This is a private apartment." She waved her hands to shoo them off like bad children. "Away now. Back to your duties, or I'll tell the captain."

The one up front grinned. She'd seen him a few times, tending to the rigging. "Oh, the captain already knows we've left our stations." He called over his shoulder. "Don't you, Captain?"

Elise heard a muffled reply, as of someone trying to shout through a gag.

"The ship is ours now, and we're collecting the full fare." He drew a knife from his belt and gestured to her collar. "Starting with that, I think. Be a good lass and take it off, now."

The little porter stuck his head in from the side. "Double

check the machine's luggage. He has fancy tools and things."

Elise did not move. "Where is my manservant?"

"He gave us some trouble, so we hung him from the yard arm. You'd better not give us any trouble either, or we'll have to—" His sentence ended with a groan as she punched him straight in the face. He stumbled back into his shouting companions, and she advanced, chasing them out of the cabin. The leader bled from his mouth, but still had his feet. He waved the knife at her. "Are you mad? We don't want to have to kill you. Just do as you're told!"

She seized the wrist of his knife-hand. "No." Her gloved fingers dug in until there was an audible crack. "You see, I suffered an accident not long ago, and since then," She hauled back and punched him in the face again, with her left hand. "not much scares me anymore."

She released him and the bleeding man slumped at the feet of his companions. Elise kicked the dropped knife away and flexed her hands, advancing on the mutineers. "My hands were damaged during that same accident, but Guissard fixed them for me. Made them stronger. He's quite clever that way." She looked up at the yard arm, where Gus swung slowly, a rope around his neck. "Aren't you, Gus dear?"

The automaton looked down at her. "Be careful, my lady."

She scoffed, turning her attention back to the sailors. "They're just men."

One of the sailors backed up to the yard arm, brandishing a cutlass. "Surrender or I'll cut the line and send your toy down to serve Davy Jones!"

She flexed her hands and slowly, ruefully shook her head. "Shouldn't have said that. You were much safer when you were just threatening me." Elise raised her hands. "But sure, I surrender. You want the collar, I'll hand it over." She brought her hands to the back of her neck, glancing up at her hanging man. "How are you doing up there?" she called. "Must be nice to have all that space to stretch your arms and legs after being cramped in the cabin."

He said nothing.

All eyes were on her. Elise slowly undid the first clasp. Behind and above them all, she saw Gus tuck his legs up, extending his tied arms down to pass beneath his feet, exposing bright metal rods. She undid the second clasp.

He snapped the ropes at his wrists and began climbing his noose, hand over hand, up to the yard arm.

Elise dropped her eyes as the last clasp clicked open. "I warn you," she said, opening the collar like a butterfly's wings. "You will wish you hadn't asked for this."

"Shut up and hand it over." The little porter snarled, extending both hands for the prize.

She brought the collar down, and the mutineers gasped as one. An ugly scar ran across her throat, just underneath her chin, sutured together with black stitches, bloodless and puckered. "Not pretty, is it?"

Something heavy landed behind them, and half the pirates turned to see the automaton straighten up, the frayed noose still around his neck.

"Now then, my love," she called. "Let us put an end to this." Elise swung the silver collar into the porter's face, chipping his other tooth.

Guissard's arms extended like stiff snakes toward two others.

* * * * *

The docking crew was surprised to see *The Uncrowned Queen* pull into port a day ahead of schedule, and doubly surprised to see that all the crew were performing their duties in manacles and leg-irons.

Once the passengers had disembarked, save two and Captain Briggs, the captain sent word into town for the nearest authority to come take his crew into custody. Many of the mutineers were bruised and battered, and one of them had twin rows of punctures in his right cheek, as if he'd been bitten by a small creature.

"You handled them mightily," Captain Briggs said to his final passengers. "If you ever desire a position as security on my vessel, or are ever in need of passage—"

Elise raised a hand. "Thank you, but no. I have had quite enough of ships for the time being. Besides," She turned and wrapped her arms around Guissard's neck. "we have a proper wedding to plan, guests or no. And still quite a journey ahead of us."

Guissard laid a gloved hand on her cheek. "And I'll be beside you. The whole way."

About the Author:

Shenoa writes from Southern California, where she lives with her brother and dancing dog. Her fanpage can be found at www.facebook.com/sbcbfiction, and she blogs at www.sbcbfiction.net

Pricilla, Mistaken Identity and Pirates

by Gary Wedlund

My credit card was stolen by a certain Pricilla Price. I'd been paying for the four hamburgers with onion rings special at White Castle when it happened. Similar-looking plastic had come back with the receipt, but I didn't realize it bore the name, Renfro L. Brown until a month later when I tried to use it again.

Once a year I got the craving for the greasy little things. I have no idea why, but it might have been the pickle. I'm just saying.

Anyway, it'd been four o'clock in the morning and my mascara had been running because Sam had just dumped me for a blonde named Doris. It'd been, "Okay, let's have sex." Then around three A.M. it'd been, "It'd be cool to break up because I met someone else a couple days ago."

I'd said, "Roll over. You're lying on my bra." When I condensed it like that it was hard to picture the bottle smashing into the wall and the neighbors standing on their porches in their bathrobes watching me run over the trash can while smoking rubber in the street.

It's likely this credit card theft was just a too-tempting opportunity for Pricilla. My name is Penni Price, a near match. She no doubt used the card without having to strip off the clear coating and change the name to an alias, which, of course, exacerbated the problems and led me to where I am today.

I mean to suggest that things got worse in a hurry.

When Pricilla penned the holdup note for the Citgo Convenience Mart robber, she used the back of her receipt for two

Admiral Feasts, seven margaritas and an extra helping of prawns at the Red Lobster down by Georgesville.

Later, when the detectives asked me about it, I blurted out, "Oh sure, I went there all the time with Sam, my boyfriend, until he made me wreck my car the night he told me about Doris. That's why all the parking tickets."

But even before that, and right after realizing I was carrying Renfro L. Brown's credit card, I'd come home to witness two pickup trucks hauling away my things. Apparently my rent checks had bounced for the second month in a row because of all the identity theft purchases—I was still a couple hours from knowing why at the time—and the manager, Ralph the Beer Balloon, had put everything I owned on the curb just to show how upset he was about having to get out of his chair.

If all the time shifts are bugging you, not to worry; just know a lot of bad things happened, and the rest will make sense. And that none of this matters anymore anyway.

The men in the pickup trucks were obviously experienced. They peeled out of the alley the moment they saw me screaming. I was out of shape and really winded by the time I got to the debris. They'd left the ratty hallway rug and that recliner I'd always hated because you had to roll off the arm rest and get off in order to push it out of recline.

Old bills flew all around. Most of those had blown against a fence, helping me round them up for the dumpster. They say that if you don't sit on the curb and rip old bills into tiny little pieces you're open to identity theft, so I did that, too, because at that time I still wasn't too sure it'd already happened. Technically, I suppose, it can happen to you twice in a row, so venting my anger on those bills was probably smart, in hindsight.

My name popped up in some Big Brother database while I was checking into the motel. Two detectives pushed through the door. They crowded me between the moment I was handing over my last paycheck and the moment I planned on asking for a room key. I recall that the room I never saw had a microwave. I left my grocery bag of ramen noodles on the clerk's table next to the fresh receipt for the first week's rent.

"Identity theft is rampant now and can get convoluted," I said from the back of car R-17, after being told about the holdup. My cuffed hands clung to the grey wire cage separating me from the men who'd told me to watch my head when they'd pushed me into the back.

"You would be a Penni Price, AKA Pricilla Price, known to frequent the Red Lobster on Georgesville, bearing a stolen credit card belonging to a Renfro L. Brown? We found your apartment empty in what appeared to be a hectic fashion. What are you in a rush to leave your neighborhood for, Miss Price?"

I sagged back into my seat and decided to wait until we got to the police station. They say they keep at you and keep at you until you confess, so it's best to not say anything, particularly on a Friday. The free lawyers never show up on a weekend. I watched those prison shows and knew the food was terrible, too. That had me fixated on ramen noodles for the first time in my entire life.

Like I said, before we got there, they mentioned the Citgo robbery and they'd already mentioned the name Pricilla, so that's how the whole thing finally dawned on me. The sky had seemed to be falling ever since Doris. And Sam wasn't worth a crap either. The rabbits deserved each other. Oh God, why does that make me want to cry?

After backing into a garage attached to the station, they dropped the door and yanked me out. We were in the hallway when two men barged through the double front doors with bags of thirty-round clips, belts of pipe bombs and blazing assault rifles. They had those little patches on their shirts, the ones with a cross and a big N under a red and blue crown. The patches looked a little like flags. I didn't realize it identified them as Aryan Nation douche-bags right way, but I figured it out during the explosions.

"Take my cold dead hand offa' my lead-hot rifle, you sons of bitchin' Hussain-lovin' bastards!" they yelled while banging away. Some people don't believe in evolution and spend their whole lives proving it hasn't happened in their part of the tree.

Their banging bullets made those zip, zip, zip sounds and instantly smacked into things. Paneling chips exploded like popcorn and papers snapped as if hit by industrial-sized rubber bands.

The detectives who were bracing me jerked a dozen times in assorted ways.

At first I thought the sprinkler system had turned on, but the spewing liquid got into my startled-open mouth. It tasted salty. When I pulled my hand away from my face, my arms were splattered with spots of red.

Next thing I knew, a bullet caught me in the chest and my backbones bounced off the sergeant's counter. I fell like a Barbie doll and jolted with a head-splitting crack onto the linoleum. Pain kept spreading within me so hard and gripping that it narrowed my vision. My heart stopped making that thumpy-thump sound in my ears, replaced by a high-pitched ringing.

Aryan Nation galoshes ran by, skating in the blood. Their owners kept shooting their thirty-round clips and tossing fizzling pipes filled with nails and powder into the secretaries and convicts. Spent cartridges tinkled everywhere. All the cops were lying in red pools in front of my eyes. I tried to move my hand out of a growing puddle of blood, but that's when they dimmed the lights on my final curtain call.

There were angels and dead relatives sharing my tunnel when the lights came back on. The relatives were fleeting parts of faces on cottonish bodies that didn't have any feet.

The angels appeared to be cutouts from a book I'd loved while in grade school. The way they wiggled back and forth like on an invisible central dowel reminded me of special effects in a low-budget fifties movie. An almost-holy song droned, "Ahhhhhhhh!" Somewhere in my head a John Wayne harmony kept saying, "Alright, copper, come in and get me. You're not taking me alive!"

This might be the perfect place to slow down some and

reflect on how I felt about someone pirating my identity. To begin with, I should have bought the internet protection plan for $9.97 a month. It probably wouldn't have helped in this case, but it's all about peace of mind and restitution.

The tunnel just went on and on, and if I had to spend eternity with some of the relatives I kept seeing out of the corners of my eyes, I'd rather have gone back, in spite of the giddy euphoria.

I felt a bit worried that the Muslims might be right. Since I'm female and every guy gets fifty virgins, the possibilities there weren't appealing. I'd ended up a crying mess just because of Doris and Sam.

Fortunately, the pearly gates materialized. I started wandering around in the grass while wearing a white gown that reminded me of a bed sheet. My sandals were the color and weight of straw, but had absolutely no sense of fashion.

There was a line to get in, which I joined out of habit. They'd set up a tent-like place, with plastic tables and folding chairs, just short of the pearly gates. Booklets and fliers had been stacked on our end. A couple ladies were asking people for their names then rummaging through card file boxes for what I suppose were reservations. Near the far end, a guy said, "Smile." He took a picture of a lady who'd finished the line. A little machine cranked out a photo ID in seconds. A teenager punched a hole in the finished ID and handed it to the woman. The woman in a long dress alligator-clipped her ID onto a shoestring necklace and put it around her neck before marching on to the gates. The double door opened a tiny bit, letting her squeeze in.

I stepped aside a moment to glare up at the top of the walls. Jerry Falwell and John Wayne were up there amongst fifty women with hairdos like Marge on the Simpsons. They were all drooling down at us with I-told-you-so stares. It's possible that this view is where the fifty virgins story came from, but I admit that's pretty convoluted.

The balding man in front of me had been looking up and down the line. "I said, 'Has a Pricilla Price arrived yet?'"

I stepped to the side so I could see down the line, too. I took off one of my drab sandals, holding it like a weapon.

Balding Man had a photo. He kept glancing at me then it, me then it, me. "What are you, deaf?"

My immediate impulse is to end my story here, but there is one irrefutable law to the universe. Life does not end at the first few layers of absurdity. Instead, life piles it on and on and on. It's maybe part of the big bang.

"My name is Penni."

"Nobody's name is Penni, Pricilla. That's the kind of dumb name a D-class, pulp-fiction writer is apt to make up out of whole cloth. And quit trying to get out from under; you've got to pay for your sins. That's our basic, number-one rule. You've been a disruptive influence upon your community."

Right about then, Ronald Reagan and Gary Cooper grabbed the man who'd just finished the line and dragged him, kicking and screaming, toward a well. "Commie bastard," Gary Cooper said.

They pitched him in to the tune of an echoing, "AAAAAHHHHHHhhhhhaa . . . aaaaaa . . . aaa . . . a . . . ." There didn't even come a splash.

A little plum of yellow smoke oozed from around the cute red roof they'd built over the well.

"No, wait, you don't understand. This woman, Pricilla Price, stole my credit card. The next thing you know—"

"Me too." Everyone but the drunk wearing the trash liner started crowding the desk, creating a mini riot.

"Alright, I'll call it in." Balding Man pushed the off-hook switch on a brick-sized cell phone with a three-foot-long antenna and Radio Shack sticker on it. Before he rotary dialed, he said, "Go wait at the end of the line, unless you want to confess and save me roaming charges."

I bit my tongue.

"Uh-huh. Uh-huh. Uh-huh," he said, but after a while he grew a scowl, put his hand over the phone, nodded to the side and said, "Go around back to the theme park. Catch the Haunted Pirate

Adventure."

* * * * *

Never mind that everyone in heaven has a hundred acre mansion. It must have been like Housewives of Atlantis in there. And it took five months, just to get around. Of course, a day is as a thousand years in the afterlife, so I'd only technically been dead a few minutes when I arrived at the turnstile.

The teenager checked me and two others for height with a marked pole. We slid into the plastic pirate boat, one to a seat, though there was room for luggage. I pulled down the safety bar securing myself into the rear. The boat casually floated into the plywood laughing-pirate-mouth water-cave entrance. There wasn't a color in the rainbow that they hadn't used while painting that.

The two other complainers in my boat were a BP gas station attendant named Jerome and Lee Harvey Oswald.

"They got the wrong guy. They framed me, saying I was the *only* shooter," Lee yelled the minute our boat paused on a little underwater conveyor belt that served as brakes. "There was this goon on a hill. When I said I was going to squeal about him being in cahoots, the CIA sent that bar owner who owed all that money to the mob to shut me up. Then they shut him up. It's not fair that I should get all the blame."

The boat wandered from one pirate scene to the next before coming to the Star Pirates space room. Luck Scallywagger got out of a triangle space fighter sporting a skull and crossbones under the pilot's window. He said to Princess Layou, "I still can't believe you're my sister."

Layou's face grew pink. She said, "You can't believe? I'm in therapy over it. While dealing with that, I let Harry get away."

"Speaking of which, must you put all your couch chat into print? I mean, think about what your comments are doing to me! I can't afford therapy as much as you. And you should be happy you don't have to resort to cartoon and video-game voiceovers."

"I was exploited and have to purge. And my hair was never better than during those movies." Layou's giant sunglasses had been propped on her forehead. She dropped them over her eyes, took a sixteen ounce sip off some drink with an umbrella in it and completely shrank into her XXXXL sweater.

"Excuse me." Lee broke the ride rule and stood in the boat, a seat up from mine. "There's been a mistake. They got the wrong guy. I wasn't the only one in Dallas, don't you know. Bush, Nixon and Edgar were there, too. What sneaky thing were they into?"

"I hate you," Layou said. "My shrink suggests I don't over-analyze and just tell people the truth. It's easier and saves on pills."

"You tell 'em, Sis."

Lee sat down and brooded.

I clapped and wolf whistled. "I thought you two were still alive? What are you doing running a ride in the afterlife?"

"There's a recession. Besides, the pirate ride isn't in heaven. It's Limbo on this side of the parking lot." Luck Scallywagger smirked. "It was either this or the next Pirates of the Caribbean movie." He looked at one hand then the other, as if still trying to figure out which was the better move for his career.

"You need to hook up with my agent," Layou said. "At least she knows her farts come out of her butt."

"What about me?" Jerome interrupted what seemed likely to be a new argument. "I've been falsely accused in a big-oil smear."

"Why do you think we can help you?" Luck asked.

"Well, you're royalty. She's a princess. You're either a prince or Dick Chaney's kid. Do you do anything practical for your futuristic peasantry, I mean, like sort out justice? Or is shooting robots and death ships all you're good for?"

"Alright, I'm game," Princess Layou said. "Did you have a good relationship with your mother?"

"I don't know what that has to do with it. I'm here because I was the lowest-paid BP employee in America. They fired me after saying I was responsible for the trillion dollar Deepwater Horizon oil spill."

"So, why did you do it?" Luck asked.

"I didn't have anything to do with the Gulf. I worked in Ohio, for God's sake. They said I left the gas cap off an SUV after a full-service fill up. The only thing that mattered, though, was how they wrote it up and colluded with a certain news source. How lame is that?"

"Well, did you leave the cap off?"

"That's hardly the point."

"Evasive," Princess Layou said. "The first part of therapy is acknowledging that you have a problem." She shook her bob of short, red hair. "He's years from recovery."

"It always comes down to a disgruntled employee." Luck cast that wise-boy-at-seventy obnoxious grin. I imagined that at a hundred and fifty he'd still look like a wrinkled little kid.

"Blow me, fly boy." Jerome shot them the finger.

Good thing that's when the ride started going because they both pulled out laser pistols. The grumpy, nearsighted bastards blew holes in the opposite wall, trying to kill us.

Jerome was alright in my book. If I'd met him before Sam, none of this would have happened. On the other hand, he was two seats up and this wasn't the Love Boat.

We still high fived across Lee's seat, but had to cut it out and sit still because a belt started taking our boat up a tall ramp. The boat was stubby, kind of like in the kiddy rides, not a proper rough-water log shape, but they sent us down a water slide anyway. We smacked into the Atlantic Ocean so hard a wave rolled over and soaked me to my panties.

A couple days later we spotted a real pirate ship. By then we'd hoisted my gown as a sail and could steer with a chunk of the seat we'd rigged as a rudder. This gave us about a half knot of headway in a gale.

The pirate ship had three masts and bristled with two rows of cannon. As it came closer, I noticed the skull and crossbones flag and the name Pirate Trouble 109 across the bow.

We came broadside at a hundred yards.

They stared us down, lined at the rail, swords in hand, muskets charged, cudgels and axes and chains dangling off meaty hands. Five or six hung in the rope ladders. One sat on a low mast, licking his lips with anticipation to pounce. They had grappling hooks and planks at the ready as their jib sails inched them closer.

Jerome wiggled free from his safety bar and stood on the boat's prow, waving. No doubt he'd make a good pirate, after the oil spill and the billionaire pirates blaming him for it.

Lee Harvey Oswald was just a coward who shot an unarmed man out of a window at a hundred yards. He didn't even belong in this story. The prick was hiding on the floor in front of his seat. We'd been wanting to pitch him over since before Star Pirates. No doubt the men of PT-109 would have him on a plank in seconds. God forbid they should lump us in with his sort.

Jerome must have had the same thought. On impulse he grabbed Oswald up out of his hiding hole. With the aid of my foot, we pitched him into the sea where the sharks who'd been following me around all my life ate all but his bobbing head in half a minute.

All the pirates laughed like they were warming to us.

I stood on the high part of the boat after that, too. I was only wearing my bra and panties, but waved with both hands, putting on a show. "Yoo-hoo! Horny pirates, yoo-hoo! Give peace a chance!"

I'd been shot by terrorists, dumped because of a blonde named Doris, and identity thieved. My landlord had put my stuff on the curb. The authorities hadn't even tried to help me, and instead had gotten me killed. Saint Peter had sent me around back without even a court hearing with the big cheese. I'm not even sure I fit in with those people behind the pearly gates. Some of them looked like idiots with a tendency to whine.

I'd never even had a chance to use the microwave oven.

The closer pirates smiled at me as the ship closed and water spit between the hulls. They sent down a rope ladder. The cook up there was having barbecue. It smelled a little like White Castle. Once a year I'm pretty much a sucker for those crazy things. It could be the dried onions.

Could a hundred-fifty horny pirates plying the eternal seas of the damned really be all that bad? In fact, I was kind of looking forward to cuddling with a man wearing hand attachments and who could say the word R employing a minute-long rumble.

After being lost at sea with someone as snarky and boring as Lee Harvey Oswald, one had needs. It was past time I joined something that appreciated me, too, and helped me take matters into my own hands, maybe swinging a cutlass and stealing a little back.

That's the other thing pirates do, don't you know?

About the Author:

Gary has a BFA from the Columbus College of Art and Design, teaching certification from Otterbein College, an MBA from the Ohio State University and a First Class FCC license earned while an electronics systems instructor for the US Army. He is employed as a Communications Systems Specialist for the City of Columbus, Ohio, and the author of the *Hidden Shaman* series.

The Child

by DH Hanni

"No. No way am I going to risk my life and my ship for a kid. A kid, Reginald! Have you lost your mind?" Naseelah said, hands perched upon her hips. She looked down upon him because her black and gold high-heeled boots made her tall, slender body even taller.

"You are so enchanting when you are indignant." Reginald smirked as his hand outlined the gold corset Naseelah wore over her black shirt. "I like these." He flicked an ornamental anchor clasp on the corset, below her left breast.

She slapped the hand away. "Not going to happen, Reginald," emphasizing his name in annoyance.

"Oh, you are mad, my sweet Naseelah. You only call me Reginald when you are upset or . . ." His grey-green eyes twinkled as his hand moved towards her rear. "in the throes of passion."

Naseelah shrugged him off and paced around the room, hoping it would deter Reginald's romantic pursuit. She folded her arms across her chest. Her gold-tipped heels clacked in measured steps on the black wooden floor of her ship, _The Aysel_.

Reginald grinned and leaned his tall, barrel-chested frame against Naseelah's desk. "I don't know why you are refusing this job. Just a moment ago you were desperate for work. Pleading you needed this job since you were blacklisted for ratting out Captain Owain to the Pirate Alliance. How the hell anyone thought that fine group of moral people was going to survive amazes me."

She sighed and looked at him askew, her eyes glowing like the two golden beacons that guarded the gate to the city of Tazos. "A kid, Reginald. Why?"

He pretended to be preoccupied, staring at the platinum ring on his left thumb. It was the Tazos Transportation and Commerce Department shield, the most important department within the city. Reginald was the top manager, allowing him to contract out delicate operations to whichever pirate he could get for cheap. Or who were desperate. And Naseelah was desperate, despite her protests.

"Does it matter, Nas? You are in no position to question the offer. You either take it or you don't. Do you have any other jobs? Plans?"

Naseelah stopped pacing. She looked around her cabin. The black paint on the walls was flaking off to the point where one could see the original oak wood. Her ragged desk, a leg beginning to rot. Her eyes softened as she thought about *The Aysel*, her true home, and the engines in grave need of repair, pondering how Marche managed to keep her in the air. Ever since the blacklisting . . . .

"That is what I thought. You need this job. You have no other choice."

"I can always say no," she answered in a less than confident voice.

"And how much do you owe? I imagine *The Aysel* can still fetch a handsome price."

Naseelah marched over to Reginald, her temper flaring up again. She grabbed his ruffled shirt. "I will never give up *The Aysel*. No amount of money or scorn could ever convince me to give her up."

Reginald grabbed her arm. "Then you have no other choice."

"I hate you," she said as she retracted her arm from his firm grasp.

"It doesn't matter how you feel about me; it's about getting the job done. Officially, the city government has no knowledge of this operation. At least it's not in any of the public documents. But the city is quite keen on getting the girl. She is . . . . Well, I'm not at much liberty to give specifics to outsiders."

Naseelah narrowed her eyes. "After all these years, and you still have the nerve to refer to me as that? I've been in the city since I was thirteen years old. Worked scrubbing the decks on the dilapidated hunk of garbage, *The Intrepid*. I may not look like a Tazos native, but I still call it home."

Reginald tensed up; the blue velvet fabric of his coat was tight across his back and shoulders. He turned his attention to a painting, pilfered, naturally, from the Grand Museum of Art in Verona. "Tazos's leaders believe the child to be of great value. I confess I myself do not know much about this most unusual cargo. She was recovered by a Tazos freight ship responding to a distress call. She was the only survivor on board. Her parents were dead as well as the crew, although no one knows why a family would be on board such a vessel. Anyway, Papa Macchini's Sinister Squad intercepted the Tazos ship and kidnapped the girl. We believe she is located within the comfortable but less than friendly confines of Macchini Castle."

"Macchini Castle?" Naseelah stared at him in disbelief.

"Yes, that one," he replied, his voice insipid. He stepped away from the picture. "I have never understood the appeal of Apraxin."

"But the Macchinis, Reg. How do you know Papa Macchini still has her?"

"The Tazos Police Intelligence Agency sent out reconnaissance balloons to the island and came back with some interesting readings."

"So how valuable can an eleven year-old girl be?"

"Very, Naseelah. This is dangerous and off the beaten path, but you are smart and unflappable." He turned around. "And may I remind you, you are in no position to turn me down. It is either this or I have *The Aysel* seized. Hard to be a pirate without a ship, is it not, Captain Naseelah?"

She said nothing but put on her shabby black frockcoat embroidered with gold and red. She glared at him as she opened the door of her quarters. "If you will excuse me, I have a ship I need to inspect."

* * * * *

"We are ready to set sail, Captain," Jacque, her first mate, said. Naseelah and Reginald stood at the front of the ebony black ship accented with gold paint around the portholes, beams, and mast on the cog ship. The shimmery gold silk sails unfurled, looking like melted butter through the wispy clouds. Reginald put a hand up to shield his eyes from the sun's glare. Despite the crisp breeze, sweat still beaded upon their skin.

"Go ahead and start the engines, Marche. I'll be in my quarters," Naseelah said, leaving Reginald at the bow. The little ship's boards rumbled as the two engines coughed before sputtering and coming to life.

Later in the day, she walked around the deck. "How are things looking?"

Jacque was reading the ship's navigation board. "Very good, Captain, although Marche and I are wondering where *The Aysel* is going. The course you've plotted for tomorrow takes us to a chain of animal sky islands. What are we picking up, Captain?"

Naseelah's smile was contrite. She hated lying to him. "I can't tell you and Marche just yet. Strict orders from Reginald and the city of Tazos." She sighed and leaned her body over the console, supporting her weight on her hands. "What I can tell you is it's an . . . unusual job at a dangerous place. Hence the small crew."

She looked out across the purple and orange swirls in the sky. Naseelah was hypnotized by them so much that without thinking, she muttered, "I hope she's worth it."

Jacque's lined tanned face—he joked that each line represented how many plunder missions he had been on—was worried. "She, Captain? Who are we going after?"

Naseelah snapped out of her reverie. Her smooth, café-brown face became angry. "What? Why do you think it's a person? She could be a ship."

Jacque remained quiet. She never barked at him like that, but a vein in Naseelah's swan-like neck pulsed, noting her increased stress level.

"Perhaps, Captain, after we have completed this job, *The Aysel* should drop you off at Bacchus Island for a week."

She laughed but it was empty, bitter. "And leave *The Aysel* to the likes of you and Marche? You might turn her into something more than an illegal freight delivery ship."

"Well, if you don't go, could I ask permission to be dropped off at Bacchus Island? Marche is acting weird. Paranoid. Keeps babbling about bad energy. Mutters about a dark end for *The Aysel.* And you."

"He's just stressed," Naseelah said, yet she was alarmed at Marche's visions. She tried to strike the fear from her mind. As Captain, she needed to stay strong, calm.

The next day, Naseelah was inputting the course for the ship when Reginald burst into the navigation cabin. "There you are woman!" His customary composed and well-dressed person was out of sorts. His blue velvet breeches were stained, the white ruffled shirt had a tear in it, he wore no frockcoat, and his hair hung in greasy strings around his face.

Naseelah kept her focus on the console. "Reginald, when you are a part of my crew, you will address me as Captain. Understood?"

Reginald huffed. "*Crew? Captain?* Is this why Jacque awoke me this morning, at the blinding crack of dawn no less, and thrust a mop and bucket at me, *Captain?*"

"Oh, yes, indeed. Did you not get the note? I left it on your pillow along with a complimentary chocolate." Naseelah got up to leave but he blocked her way. "I don't have time for this. Move out of the way."

Reginald remained rigid.

"Reginald, as Captain of *The Aysel*, I am ordering you to get out of my way and return to your assigned duty. I have to help Marche with an engine." She placed a hand upon the translucent handle of her pistol.

"If I don't comply, what are you going to do, Captain? Shoot me with one of those electrified bullets? I'm with the Tazos city government! One of its top people! You can't kill me!"

"You stupid bastard. Who said anything about killing you?" She shot a small pellet of electricity encased in lead into his foot, snapping the buckle off the shoe. He yelped, grabbing the injured foot. He bounced on the other one while yelling obscenities at her as she left.

* * * * *

"Captain," Marche addressed Naseelah, who was at the bow. A brisk wind whipped her hair like a curtain floating in the night sky, "I see we are headed toward Chariot." The little man approached her, lacing and unlacing his hands. Even though he had been aboard *The Aysel* and under her captaincy for several years, the Amazonian beauty still generated nervousness within him.

"Yes, Marche, we are headed there. What of it?" Naseelah pushed the tip of the skull's nose on her compass watch and watched the electric hands point northwest.

"Well, Captain, um, well, Jacque and me were wondering where we are going? I don't know of anything we would be retrieving from Chariot. I mean, it's just an agricultural sky island." His words were rushed.

"We aren't going there, my dear little Marche." She closed the compass watch and turned to him. The man's smile was docile, but he averted her gaze, choosing instead to stare at the ground.

"Then where are we going, Captain? I keep seeing . . . things. Dark things."

She was uneasy. The hair on the back of her neck bristled with energy. "Marche, just worry about keeping *The Aysel* in the air. Leave our destination to me. I trust you and you trust me, right?" She didn't wait for his response. "So just get back to work.

There aren't enough of us to waste time on idle chatter."

Marche lifted his head, puzzled as he watched Naseelah disappear below deck.

That evening, the foursome gathered in *The Aysel's* large dining room, the lack of a significant crew echoed in each word they spoke. Gathered at one end of the mahogany table, Naseelah sat at her customary spot at the head. To her right sat Jacque and Marche to her left. Reginald scurried from the kitchen to the dining room to serve them, still wearing the clothes from the first day. They were a mess of wine, burnt cream sauces, and grease from cleaning the ship.

Naseelah soon discovered such a refined palette as Reginald's did not translate into actual cooking ability. His fingers showed numerous cuts. There was a dirty bandage upon the tip of his left middle finger from where he'd sliced it off while preparing dinner one night. He hadn't been able to locate it until Marche found it in his soup.

"Reg, please sit down. We've got plenty of time for dinner," Naseelah said in a soft voice. Reginald flopped into a chair, limbs splayed out, his face slack.

The Aysel jostled them as they passed through a violent thunderstorm. They held onto the table, which was bolted down, to prevent them from crashing into the wall. Well, all except Reginald who didn't seem to mind as his chair knocked him about.

"Jacque, Marche, I have been vague about our course and job, on purpose. Reginald approached me with an unofficial request by the city of Tazos. There is something very valuable the city wants. Or rather *someone* the city wants."

"Someone, Captain?" Marche interrupted. "Since when do governments employ pirates to retrieve people?"

"When that person is of some importance and power," Reginald uttered in a dead tone.

"Captain?" Marche said. He and Jacque alternated looks from her to Reginald.

"Tazos wants us to retrieve a little girl from Macchini Castle. She—"

"Macchini Castle? You mean the one owned by Papa Macchini, the man who obliterated the Burtons, destroyed all of the Tableau chain of sky islands?" Jacque asked.

"Yes, the same. Now, as—"

"Captain, you know I respect you, love you as I love *The Aysel*, but this is a suicide mission!" Jacque rose from his chair. "We—"

In the same drained voice, Reginald said, "The girl has a power the Tazos government feels would be best exploited by a benevolent force rather than a malevolent one." He closed his eyes and leaned his head against the chair.

"And what power is that?" Jacque asked Naseelah.

She shot a quick glance at Reginald. "I don't know. That information hasn't been shared. Yet."

Eyes still closed, Reginald replied. "She's a telepath, or so the rumor goes. A very influential one. She's more valuable for her ability to get people to do what she wants rather than being able to read minds. The government wants to place her into an appropriate home situation. An orphan, the only survivor of an exploration ship which crashed onto one of the sky islands on the furthest reaches of our universe.

"She was recovered by a Tazos freight ship. According to the captain's log, the girl quickly demonstrated extraordinary abilities to manipulate thought and actions. Before she could be delivered safely to Tazos, the freight ship was overtaken by Macchini's Sinister Squad. We believe they must have cracked the encryption the ship's communication was relayed on." He let out a long tired sigh.

"So how does Tazos know it was the Sinister Squad?" Jacque asked.

"The trademark SS was carved onto the cheeks of the dead," Naseelah ventured.

"You are correct, Captain," Reginald said.

No one talked or moved. Naseelah wondered if Reginald had fallen asleep before his eyes fluttered open. He stood up. "I must get the dessert out," he mumbled as he shuffled toward the kitchen.

"Sit, Reg." She got up and directed him to her empty chair. She began pacing, tinkering with an anchor clasp on the corset.

"We should turn around. And now, Captain. This is a suicide mission. We'll end up with SS carved on us," Marche pointed out. He laced and unlaced his fingers. "This must be what I keep seeing."

Jacque shifted his eyes away from Marche. "How much did you accept for this job, Captain? How much are our lives worth to you?" He got up and stood in Naseelah's path.

Her face remained stoic as she absorbed his furious face. "Not as much as I had hoped."

Jacque was ready to explode, but the frosty stare she gave him made him reconsider his next course of action.

"The blame is not entirely hers," Reginald said. "Your captain was in no position to refuse. Not unless she wished to be killed for knowing too much. The city does not want this to be made known to the world. You could see how it could be misconstrued."

"So our lives mean little?" Jacque asked him.

"We won't die, Jacque. Haven't lost a crew member in all these years," Naseelah pointed out as she moved away from her first mate and most trusted friend.

"Thank you for the reassurance, Captain," his tone caustic. "Guess you were right, Marche." He sat down and drowned the sour wine in his cup.

Marche spoke up: "Captain, how are we to get into Macchini Castle? As soon as we approach the island, its defense system will be alerted, and they'll send out the air hounds. If we're lucky."

"I've been thinking about that. There's got to be a way around their defense system. It will only activate if we are picked up by their radar? And don't radar systems only scan above an object or at the same level?" Naseelah asked.

Marche was cautious in his answer. "True, Captain."

"So it doesn't pick up anything if the object is below, right? Isn't that how we were attacked by *The Rogue Red* a while back?" Naseelah said, a gleam of hope in her gold eyes.

"You're right, Captain. Our radar didn't pick them up. It's why I requested all the extra equipment and had us docked for two months while I reconfigured it," Marche said.

"Do you think Macchini's system is set up like ours?" Excitement fluttered across her face, spreading to infect Jacque and Reginald like scurvy.

"Of course not, Captain. You remember how long it took me to configure it. And only after I talked to my buddies on other ships. No, no way Macchini's defense system has the same set up."

"Is there a way to be absolutely certain?" she asked.

"Oh yes. All I have to do is launch some phantom cannon balls at Macchini Castle. I'll launch a couple from underneath the island. If no air hounds come out to play, we would be good to go."

"Captain, I still think this is too dangerous," Jacque interjected. "We just don't have the crew. We don't even have a map. Does anyone know where this girl is?"

Still exhausted, Reginald found a second wind and sat up alert. "I have a map. Courtesy of Command Inspector Busko. Admittedly it is a few years old, but from all the reconnaissance balloons we've sent out, it doesn't appear much has changed."

* * * * *

The Aysel docked several meters under Macchini Castle. The ship was well hidden due to a dark, massive rain storm swirling around the island. An occasional thunder rumble and flash of purple lightening created an eerie glow. Marche was ordered to stay on the ship with strict word from Captain Naseelah to leave, no questions asked, should Reginald, Jacque, or she be captured, wounded, or killed. All three were equipped with pistols loaded with electric bullets, although Jacque insisted upon bringing a traditional shotgun as well. Reginald had to be talked out of wearing his Tazos ornamental platinum sword. It had broken into two pieces as soon as Jacque attempted to put an edge to the blade.

After testing the radar system, Marche created a hole in the castle's underbelly, somewhere near the holding cells, according to Reginald's map. Using a grappling hook, they climbed in from *The Aysel*. Jacque marked their spot with linseed oil, which would glow under the portable black light he carried in a satchel. Every ten feet they walked, he dropped a few drops of oil so they would be able to hurry back to the ship.

Naseelah had eschewed her high-heeled boots for a pair of well-worn, flat-footed black leather boots and the trio silently crept along the granite corridor. A single beam from a flameless candle lit their way. Water trickled down a wall, making the chilly air damp and reek of mildew. The chatter of mice and rats were the only noises.

"Are you sure this is the dungeon, Reg?" Naseelah whispered. They were at the end of one corridor. She looked left then right. "Which way do we go now?"

Reginald pulled out the map and shone the light on it. "According to the map, we should take a right, follow the corridor until we've passed the second malachite inlaid gate. Once we reach it, there should be four silver monkeys. We want to pick the monkey with the ruby eyes. It opens the gate."

"Jacque, mark an X here so we know this is the hallway we want to return to," Naseelah said. While Jacque drew an X with his finger dipped in the linseed oil, she turned to Reginald. "It's been too easy, Reg. Are you sure the little girl is going to be behind the gate? What if Macchini's moved her?"

"According to Command Inspector Busko, Macchini imprisons all people he deems special in the room behind the monkey gate."

Naseelah looked down the corridor. "If she is so important,

why aren't there any guards?"

Reginald furrowed his brow briefly as he paused to think. "Perhaps the gate isn't the main entrance to the cell. The map says another series of corridors lie beyond it. There may be guards there."

"Done, Captain," Jacque said.

With a nod she led them down the corridor to the malachite gate. The silver monkey with the ruby eyes was the second from the left, and as she pressed it, a horrible, screeching cry pierced the dead air. They jumped back from the gate, Jacque and Naseelah with their pistols ready to fire, as the gate retracted into the floor. Reginald covered his ears. The alarm continued, yet no one heard the thunder of footsteps, no shouts of guards, nothing to indicate anyone had been alerted to their presence.

The alarm ceased, but Naseelah hesitated before signaling to proceed. While the air in the corridor had been cold enough for them to see their breath, the air past the monkey gate was humid and tropical.

Naseelah and Jacque were acclimated to heat, but sweat already percolated on Reginald's brow as he held out the map. He fanned himself. "How can it be dark and so hot at the same time? We go straight for 1500 yards. There should be a carved parrot on the right side. Press on it, and it leads to a large room, presumably where the girl is."

Jacque squinted down the hallway. "I don't see anybody down there. Why wouldn't Macchini post guards?"

Naseelah was unsettled by Jacque's observation. It reinforced a nagging seed of doubt which had been germinating from the time they'd broken into the castle. Things had been easy. Too easy and too quiet. If this girl was as powerful and as precious as Reginald claimed, where was all the protection?

I don't need protection, a faint and ethereal voice said.

Naseelah noticed no reaction to the voice from Jacque or Reginald. She dismissed it as some wild thought brought on by stress.

Down the corridor they walked. The air became dense and stagnant. Reginald wheezed, his footsteps becoming fainter, his position falling further and further behind. By the time Naseelah and Jacque reached the carved parrot door, both had a strong earthy smell. They waited for Reginald to catch up, taking the opportunity to catch their own breath.

I need no interference from outsiders.

"Did you hear that, Jacque?" Naseelah whispered.

"Hear what, Captain?" he gasped as he leaned against the wall.

"The voice. Soft and floaty. Like a child's voice. You can't hear it echoing off the walls?"

Before he could reply, Reginald crawled toward them. "The voice . . ." he began but stopped and dry heaved.

"Reginald!" Naseelah exclaimed. Jacque and she lifted him up and leaned him against the wall. "Reg, you heard the voice, too! What did she say?"

"Go . . . away. Leave me. Leave me, Naseelah," he gasped. His face was pale and dirty, his lips void of all color. "She's . . ." He clawed at his throat, gagging. His grey-green eyes bulged, the blood vessels visible in the whites. His face turned red, like he was sunburnt, and his tongue lolled out. Naseelah yanked on his hands, unable to pry them off.

"Help, Jacque!" she commanded, yet even with the grizzled man's help, Reginald's hands still remained upon his neck. He went from red to blue to white before no more sounds came out. He sat frozen and rigid.

See. I have no need for protection.

Naseelah shuddered. She thought back to Marche's words. There's no way he can be right, she thought. She took deep breaths to calm herself down. This could all be a trick perpetrated by Papa Macchini. Some kind of warning device. But then how to explain Reginald's death?

Naseelah looked at Jacque. He started to open his mouth, but she didn't hesitate. "Go! Get back to *The Aysel* and leave immediately!" she ordered.

"Captain, I. I can't leave you." Jacque hand's shook as he held the gun, the barrel trembled.

"You are commanded to return to the ship. Go, now!" She cocked the pistol at him, finger on the trigger, but her hand, too, shook and tears mixed with sweat stung her eyes.

Jacque saluted. "Yes, Captain. Take my shotgun and the black light." He started to hand the two items over.

"No. Keep those. You may need them more than I will. Now, go!" She motioned the gun down the hallway.

"Aye, aye, Captain!" Jacque hesitated a moment before turning down the hall. He ran until Naseelah could no longer see him.

Follow the light.

Naseelah turned and saw a green pulsating ball of light floating in front of her.

"Are you the girl we came here for?" she called out. The green light began moving away and up a spiral staircase, but Naseelah did not move.

I need no protection. Your reasons for coming here confuse me.

"We . . . I was led to believe you had been kidnapped by Papa Macchini. He's a dangerous man. We . . . I am here to rescue you from him."

Rescue me? I'm in no danger from him and neither are you. If you do as I ask.

The green ball of light paused and came back. It waited for Naseelah to move, but she remained in place until a placid invisible force pushed her forward. She resisted, but the force shoved her. A jolt of pain seized her muscles, causing her to stumble forward and up the staircase.

The staircase ended and exposed a great hall. It was the length of ten *Aysels* and as high as 15. Naseelah stopped and stood in wonder. In the middle, upon a marble dais encased in a spherical blue force field, sat a beautiful girl. She had long, wavy brown hair, crystal blue eyes, a perfect symmetrical face with a pert nose, and rosy lips. She was the picture of serenity. The child was surrounded by Macchini's Sinister Squad, all clad in blood red, as they just stood there in five neat rows, six people deep. They wore no weapons and their eyes shone glossy black. And vacant. Naseelah looked around the great hall for Papa Macchini, a man she had fortunately never encountered, but legend said he was short with Earth Aryan looks.

Father will be here soon. Please have a seat, Captain Naseelah.

A large white pillow appeared. Before she could protest, Naseelah was lifted by members of the Sinister Squad and seated upon the pillow.

"Father? How do you know my name? Who are you?" the words rushed from Naseelah's mouth. Her heart beat at a rate only matched by the RPMs of *The Aysel*'s engines. Her head swung around, searching for an escape.

You will not be leaving, Naseelah. What a pretty name Naseelah is. It means zephyr, cool breeze, doesn't it?

Naseelah floated closer to the little girl.

I am quite happy to complete my family.

"Your family?" Naseelah choked out. "What are you?"

I am what your lover Reginald informed you I am. But I do not desire to go to Tazos. I do not desire to be used by anyone anymore.

A small, corpulent, seated, male figure glided beside Naseelah. His blonde hair was parted down the middle and seemed glued to his head. He stared straight ahead, his eyes the same glossy black as the Sinister Squad. "Good morning, my Child," he said in a pleasant robotic voice.

Good morning, Father. I have brought Mother. Isn't she lovely, Father?

Papa Macchini turned to his left. A false smile plastered on heavy face. "She is indeed lovely, my Child," he said and turned back to the girl.

"Let me go. Let me return to my ship." Naseelah was panicky and made a move to get up, but as she stood, a sharp pain—like thousands of small knives—pierced her spine. She cried out and collapsed back onto the pillow.

That was most unwise, Mother. Father did the same thing. Several times. But you see how well he is doing now, the Child uttered in a soothing voice.

Between gasps of pain, Naseelah replied, "I will not be like him. Return me to my ship. I promise not to tell anyone. I promise not to say anything about this place."

You are a pirate, are you not, Mother? I cannot possibly trust you nor can I allow you to leave. You have no ship to return to, anyway. The Aysel has been destroyed; the remainder of your crew is dead.

Naseelah bolted up again. Her spine seized in pain again. Her legs wobbled and buckled. "NO, NO, NO!" Feeling flowed out of her legs. She watched as they twisted before her body sunk down onto the silk pillow. Using her arms, she tried to disentangle them but something flung her arms away. Naseelah felt no pain, was in too much shock, as her legs contorted into a cross-leg position.

"Did you . . . do this to me?" she whispered.

The Child's gaze remained pleasant. Yes, Mother, I have. I told you I did not desire to be controlled anymore.

She stood and walked to Naseelah, her feet floating on air. She came eye-level to Naseelah. Without ever moving her cherry lips, the Child continued. *My old parents controlled me too much. Once they discovered my abilities, they made me do bad things to bad people. To good people, too. They got greedy and offered me to whoever would give them the most money. It is how your lover found out about me. Father here sent word that he had a very special possession.*

"But, the freight ship. Your parents." Naseelah felt sick and her head spun. The words of the Child, the nature of the situation, Reginald's story, Marche's words, began to snap into place.

She was frightened of the Child. "You were behind your

parents' deaths."

The Child's smile grew bigger. Mother, you are so smart! Much smarter than Father. Father had to be shown the truth.

Naseelah shuddered in the shadow of the Child's praise.

You need not be afraid, Mother. I can tell you are much stronger than Father. It took him much effort to see me as his Child.

The Child looked at Papa Macchini. Father, show Mother the effort it took to make you love me.

Papa Macchini removed his jacket and shirt. His pillow floated next to the Child. Naseelah began to look away, refusing to meet either of their eyes, but the same invisible entity that had forced her into the room pushed her face to view Papa Macchini.

Mother, you must look. You must. You must see what will happen to you if you do not accept my love.

"Punishment does not make someone love you."

My parents believed it did. Come, look Mother.

Naseelah shut her eyes, still refusing. "If your parents punished you, why would you desire to hurt others to make them love you?"

I loved my parents, Mother. When I did what they asked, they did not hurt me. They ignored me. Left me alone while they enjoyed life. But when I refused, they would beat me and tell me it was because they loved me. They would pay more attention to me when I was bad. I wanted them to love me.

I do not wish to harm you, Mother. That is why I ask you to look at Father's body.

Naseelah's eyes were pried open to stare at his body. It looked as if a rabid animal had clawed the flesh. Some of the wounds were still pink while others festered and smelled rotten. The stench wafted to Naseelah, and she swallowed the bile which had bubbled from her stomach. Perhaps if she complied with the Child, she may be able to escape.

You will not be leaving. The child's voice interrupted Naseelah's thoughts.

She faced the Child again. The pleasant smile disappeared. The Child's eyes had turned into two spinning orbs of storm; steel grey and swirling. Her angelic face was now a grimace of hate.

Such thoughts are not permitted, Mother. How can a Mother wish to leave her Child?

Before Naseelah could respond, her head began to ache, like a giant squeezing her head in between his hands. Flashes of her past spun before her. The memories of her own lost family. Her teenage years spent on various ships flying the skies in search of booty. The memory of killing the former Captain of *The Aysel* in a mutiny. Everybody and everything she had ever done swirled away as the hurricane of life emptied her head. Naseelah clawed at the air, hoping to grasp and cling to those memories, to those people but the memories flew away.

Her body jerked like a puppet on a string. She whimpered and gave up.

Naseelah felt a blanket of calm spread over her. An ethereal contentment cloaked her heart. Her mind was light. At ease. Free from the restraints of thought and replaced with the hot sensation of love.

The Child, her Child, her beautiful, clever Child, smiled at her.

Naseelah beamed with pride. Happy tears emerged from the corners of her now black eyes.

About the Author:

DH Hanni enjoys historical fiction, fantasy, and anything with great characters and a compelling story. New to the world of writing but not reading, *The Child* is the first published work by the author. DH Hanni currently lives in Eastern Washington (state).

The Price of Victory

by Kerry Lynne

There is no sound louder than the sound of silence, especially after the crash of a sea battle. Guns roaring, pistols cracking, the clash of swords and the shouts of men all fall away into a deafening nothing.

A fortnight ago, Cate Mackenzie had been kidnapped by Captain Nathanael Blackthorne of the feared pirate ship the *Ciara Morganse*, the very pirates she now walked among. She had been both shocked and relieved aboard the *Morganse*. The shock had stemmed from not being chained or confined. After all it was a ship; where was she to go? One woman against 200 pirates was slim odds, even with the pistol she had been handed.

The relief had come after finding a reason to no longer wish to be rescued.

As the Morganse had swung into her position, the privateer Nightingale bearing down on her, Nathan had sent Cate Mackenzie to the hold, brooking no argument that she was to go as far forward as possible and stay. He shoved a pistol in her hand, with the brusque instructions of "Save this for yourself." A pat on the shoulder, and she had been sent on her way.

Down the companionway she went. 'Tween decks was chaos, but an organized one. Muskets and cutlasses were dispersed, while strips of cloth were secured around heads, arms, or waists, to differentiate themselves from the enemy if it came to hand-to-hand fighting. Tubs of slow-match and baskets of cartridges poured up from the hold, while wet sand was spread against slippage in the inevitable blood. Over the din was heard the rap of the carpenter and his mates' hammers, for "clear the decks" meant not only stowing every object which might pose a hazard, but knocking down the cabin walls.

Cate hung onto the manrope to keep from being bowled over by the hands racing up and down the companionway with laden arms. At the bottom of the steps, she balked. The hold was dark and airless, smelling of things gone too wet for too long. What checkered light that managed to squeeze through the grates died within a few paces. She turned away from the stream of men, toward the bow. Clutching the pistol, sliding one foot in front of the other, she groped her way past casks, hogsheads, bales, and crates. Each step took her farther from the furor of preparation, and the comfort of human voices faded. She thought a few times she had reached her destination, only to discover it was a barrel or some other obstacle.

At last, a blind hand verified a solid wall before her. The ship veered and lurched. She skidded on the wet boards and came down hard on one knee. Swearing away the pain, she crawled to the wall and planted her back against it, ignoring the wet coming up through the planks and soaking her breeches.

All further thoughts were blotted out by the first gun blast, another seconds after, followed by a rolling sequence from fore to aft. The reverberations clashed into each other and settled in her bones. Cannon was nothing new to her. Those experienced before, however, had been with land under her feet and a husband at her side. She knew little of sea battles. Piercing 12 inches of oak wasn't unthinkable, dooming them all to a watery death. She tried to convince herself that she should find courage in those guns: they were the Morganse's defense, their safety in every bone-rattling burst.

The splintering crash of the Morganse taking her first hit dissolved all resolution. Cate felt the ship shudder through the wood at her back. The Morganse sagged, but then came up on the swell, rising above the pain, and fired. The timbers creaked under the strain, flinching at every hit. It became a hypnotic din: the guns' roar, the crash as they leapt back against their tackles, the bellow of men and rumble of carriages being hauled back into place.

Roar. Bellow. Rumble. Roar. Bellow. Rumble . . . It was a three-beat tempo from a 36-piece orchestra.

Fingers of fear crawled up like the wetness at Cate's bottom. The water seemed to jet higher between the planks with every roll of the ship. The waves rushing past the hull sounded too much like water over a falls, pouring in, the ship becoming nothing more than a coffin. The acrid smell of gunpowder overpowered the hold's dankness. On the smoke rode the shrieks of the wounded and dying, and the smell of blood. It seemed impossible that anyone could remain alive in the face of all the gunfire.

The deck pitched as the Morganse carved another turn. The thud of the great guns gave way to the staccato crackle of small arms: muskets and pistols. The barrages were a pummeling assault, one lethal wave overlapping the next. The ship slowed. Then came the grind and scrape of wood against wood, like two gigantic tubs, the bulkhead at Cate's back reverberating. All sense of motion ended. The musket fire intensified. Deafened by the guns, she could barely make out what sounded almost like an infantry charge: the cries of men, the clash of swords, and sporadic pop of pistols.

And then, it was quiet.

It brought no sense of peace. If Cate had been scared before, she was terrified now. She wished she knew more of what constituted victory at sea. On land, it was often a matter of which side took the fewer casualties or gained the most ground. Was it a simple matter of which ship was still afloat, which captain still stood, or were there other deciding factors? She clutched the pistol and waited. Joints aching, hand cramping, time became interminable, marked off by her shuddering gasps from holding her breath while striving to listen.

Having wished for the sight for so long, when the lantern appeared, she thought the glow through the gloom and smoke to be a dream. Unsure if it was friend or foe, she cowered against the bulkhead, clasping a hand to her mouth lest the rasp of her breathing reveal her location. There was nothing to be done for her heart, hammering so loudly, it was sure to give her away.

"Hoy! Missus?" came a voice through the dark. "By yer leave!"

And then, the light disappeared.

Rising stiffly, Cate groped a return path, the fogged light through the grates and the cries of agony her beacon. Finding the steps at last, she came up to the gun deck into an ethereal world. The sun streamed through the ports in glaring shafts through whorls of grey smoke, the men moving like dark ghosts. From the swirling clouds came voices, thickened and muffled, orders colliding with pleas. She came upon a wounded man leaned against a gun carriage. As she knelt, she was caught by the arm.

"He's gone," the pirate shouted, still deafened by gunfire. His smoke-blackened face pinched with grief as he looked down at his fallen mate.

Her ears still ringing, it took Cate a moment to fully understand what he had said. Her first impulse was to argue, but then saw his meaning. The man sat clutching his abdomen. A shard of wood, nearly the thickness of his arm, had speared him. As his life oozed between his fingers, he wore the shocked look of one knowing he was about to die and naught to be done about it. Another, sprawled nearby, had been taken by a more merciful means, half of his head cleanly swept away.

Wiping her eyes, now burning from the smoke, Cate climbed to the main deck, the dread of what she might find weighting every step.

The first of her prayers had been answered: the *Morganse* still swam.

The second remained to be seen.

On deck, the last rays of afternoon slanted on damage that was far worse than below. Hanging shoulder-high, the smoke shrouded anyone standing, giving them a ghastly headless appearance. Cate had seen the havoc wrought by a cannonball on an open battlefield. It was nothing compared to what 18 pounds of hurtled iron could do, smashing through everything—and everyone—in its path: shredded canvas, splintered wood, and snarled rope, the shattered bodies resembling half-butchered hogs. Two gun ports had been blown into one.

As before the battle, it was a scene of chaos, but again with purpose. The wreckage of rigging and spars was already being cut away and tossed overboard, along with the bodies past identification. These mariners bore the added pain of the damage suffered upon their ship, a lady who had fought as valiantly as they. The powerful voices of the captains of the tops, forecastle, waist, and the like, rallied their men. The pirates busied with tending each other, tying rags about bloodied limbs and heads. Some sat stoically as their mates fished into their flesh with a knife for whatever battle had inserted. The more seriously injured lay waiting, either for help or to die.

The price of victory.

Cate's bare toes curled in her shoes as she picked her way through the destruction, the planks treacherously slippery with blood. The blood ran in glistening red streams toward the scuppers, the sea taking on a brackish pink cast. She closed her ears as she passed the gurgling coughs and death rattles. Tiptoeing through offal and vomit, she felt something round and slightly giving underfoot. She looked down to see a fingertip sticking out from beneath her foot. More could be seen lying about, single knuckles to entire digits, with the occasional pinkish curve of an ear. She inquired time and again as to the whereabouts of the Captain. No one knew. Finally, a man mutely gestured toward the other ship.

The two ships sat gaffed together, planks rigged between the rails. Ravaged and listing badly, the Nightingale was a sorry sight. Mainmast splintered, yards tangled, shredded canvas draped from her waist to nearly her bow. Wallowing on the swell, she slumped in the water, her spirit as shattered as her rigging.

Cate hesitated, apprehensive as to what Nathan would say to her crossing to the other ship. Concern dissolved any fear of admonishments. Hitching her skirts, she climbed up on the rail and slithering her way on a plank across the open space. She gave a huge sigh of relief when her feet touched the solidness of the Nightingale's deck.

Smoke hung even heavier there, the smell of blood and death stronger still. Cate made her way down the deck, the soft grind of sand and squelch of blood underfoot joined by the crunch of shattered glass, spread to defend against boarders. Damaged as she may have been, the Morganse had her revenge. Her chain shot had found the Nightingale's masts, severing both. One had fallen across onto the Morganse's rail; many of the hands using it as a bridge. The other dangled at an acute angle into the sea. The Nightingale's flag sagged from its broken halyard, soaking in the blood of her crew. A soft flapping noise drew Cate's attention to the Morganse's colors, still on display, the winged and haloed skull smiling down on its victim.

Morgansers were scattered about. One seemed to recall seeing the Captain somewhere astern. Scrabbling over the downed mast, and the tangle of canvas and ropes, she finally came across a truly familiar and comforting face, Pryce, the Morganse's Quartermaster. Wherever he was, his Captain wouldn't be far away.

Pryce straightened from tending an injured man. Rivulets of sweat made white streaks in the soot which blackened his face and chest, rendering him to look like some kind of odd zebra.

"I thought I saw him a-makin' his way aft," he said in his West Country rumble. He gestured in that direction with a bloodied hand. Whether the blood was his, or from the casualty at his feet, she couldn't tell.

Pryce had been correct. Cate's heart lightened at seeing Nathan on the afterdeck, propped against the binnacle. He sat in a pool of blood, his legs splayed in front of him. His arms hung limp at his sides, his sword still gripped in one hand. His shirt had been reduced to a collection of linen ribbons, glistening and bright red. His chest and arms were gashed to the point of crisscrossing, rendering him red from his waist down. Blood ran from the side of his face, dripping from the point of his beard.

"Nathan." She fell to her knees next to him, slipping in the blood. "Nathan!"

It took a few moments, but Nathan finally broke his blank stare to focus on her. A weak smile spread slowly across the smoke-blackened face. Gasping, he attempted to speak. He gulped and tried again. "Hello, luv," he said in a hoarse rasp. "Are ye all right?"

"God, Nathan." She sputtered, starting to scold him. Then she saw the sincere concern in his eyes. She bit her lip "Yes, I'm fine."

He lifted his head to look about the deck, but let it fall back an instant later. "Looks like the swabbers will have a grand task."

His dark eyes shifted to hers, his brow furrowing. "You're sure you're well?"

His image shimmered as tears began to well in her eyes. "I'm fine, but I think we might consider getting you back aboard."

Nathan looked about himself, puzzled. "Perhaps you should see to the others first." He closed his eyes, his chest rising and falling. A faint wet rattling sound accompanied each gasp for air.

Cate turned her head. It wasn't a good sign: he didn't even realize he was injured. The benefit was he seemed to suffer no pain, but even that was a bad sign, a very bad sign.

"Ah, ye found him, Sir." Pryce squatted down and gave his Captain a critical eye. "'Pears we need to get him to his cabin."

"Let's try to stop some of this bleeding—" Cate began, ripping strips from her shift for bandages as Pryce sat Nathan up. The movement caused him to cough, blood trickling from the corner of his mouth.

"Suffering Christ!" Pryce murmured while peering at Nathan's back. "Burn and sink me, he's been shot."

Cate swore, steeled herself, and ripped faster.

Nathan coughed again, spatters of blood speckling his lips.

"Perhaps we should just take him to the captain's cabin

here."

Pryce didn't hesitate: "Nay, he'll fare better when he's on his own ship."

In preparation to move him, Cate tried to take Nathan's sword, but his fist wouldn't give way.

"Nathan," she called, quietly. There was no response, his gaze locked somewhere in front of him. "Nathan!"

Nothing.

Laying a hand to his cheek, she tipped his head carefully toward her.

He blinked, tried to smile.

"Let go of your sword, Nathan," she urged, tugging gently. "I'll mind it for you."

Nathan's fingers twitched, but failed to open. His grip, however, lessened enough for her to pull it free. She laid it reverently on the deck, where he could see it.

Pryce rose to his feet. "You!" he bellowed to two nearby hands. "Yes, you couple o' ill-begotten scupperlouts! Haul your sorry carcasses over here and bear a hand!"

Blackened and disheveled, the two exchanged startled looks. "But we're Nightingales," one finally said.

What could be seen of Pryce's face flushed. "By the Devil's horns and tail, yer Morgansers and members o' the Brethren now. Clap on to yer Cap'n here and lean into it like yer bein' paid for it!"

Knuckling their foreheads like two whipped puppies, the pair bent to help. Cate quickly bound the worst of Nathan's wounds. A few times, he drew a breath, as if to say something, but hadn't the strength. Instead, he kept his eyes fixed on Cate's face, a lifeline to a drowning man. His gaze was still fixed on her as his arms were slung over the men's shoulders, and he was lifted to his feet. He blenched then his eyes rolled back, unconscious.

"Probably just as well," muttered Pryce. "Move along, you gallowsy sluggards."

Cate stooped to retrieve the sword from the deck and

followed the small procession through the swirling smoke, back to the Morganse.

About the Author:

Kerry was a history major in college and went into teaching. That didn't work, so she had two office careers. That didn't work either. Through a circuitous sequence of events, she wound up in the decorative painting world, where she travel taught and published for some 30 years. And then, her hand wouldn't work. So she went back to what she knew: writing, history and sailing. It remains to be seen if that is working.

For further adventures with Cate Mackenzie, Mr. Pryce, and Captain Nathanael Blackthorne, look for "*The Pirate Captain, Chronicles of a Legend*" available at Amazon or other sources for print or ebook.

Death and The Fish Bowl Pontoon

by Sheri Harper

Death strikes like a viper, bang.

I learned this the hard way after twenty years of marriage. You're bit: My husband passed on the news of his cancer after his yearly physical. The poison spreads: Six long and short weeks while the radiation burns, churns and the chemical stew and the surgery, well, you've heard. You spend time at the hospital. Then like a rattler slipping into the weeds, a white sheet hid my husband's face forever.

I wandered down south like so many others and attempted to find someone, some thing, that would fill the emptiness. Grief weighted every step. I found beach after beach on which I hid from sunburn while clinging to umbrella dark like I'd become a night shade, dimly fighting to make sense out of what I could make out in the numb blaze of day.

Because Rubio Hernan stepped on my foot trying to hand me his sales brochure I actually spoke to someone besides my children. A man like Rubio, with hair matted with grease and gold chains at the neck, wearing cowboy boots on the beach—you know the type—is one you normally avoid.

I said thank you and turned over.

"Yo, senorita. Don't turn your back. This is the perfect answer to low-cost waterfront property. Really. They're selling like hotcakes. Think about it."

My pain showed in my uplifted eyebrow, I hoped. "Uh-uh, not for me."

His smile exposed gold crowns. "Come on, give it a try? What do you have to lose?"

I shook my head, looking up the beach. What did I have to

lose? Tears brimmed at my eyes.

A jingling of keys sounded. Next thing I knew, he knelt beside me, shoving a brochure under my hand. "Come on. Three o'clock today. At the marina. Just take a look."

I slammed a fist on the brochure, partly to threaten him, partly to keep the paper from littering. "Fine. I've got it. Just go, leave me alone."

"Hey, hey, I can take a hint. But think it over. I only have five left. Three o'clock. I know I'll be seeing you."

You're probably thinking, oh, no, she didn't have an affair with the guy, did she?

No. I didn't. At least not the way you think. I might have been lonely, but I wasn't that low.

Moments later, he yelled down the beach. "I have an inexpensive used model. Great price. Come check it out."

I'm a sucker for a good deal, so let's just say, I soon adjusted to my life in a fishbowl.

At three o'clock that day Rubio showed me around the one room solar-powered vehicle. It had a cooking surface on the fold-out solar lounge. It had a solar-powered water exchange unit (it had a mini-nuke backup that I had to have serviced every two years, along with an ocean-powered generator for random needs). I could bathe whenever I wanted on the solar lounge, water running to the drain on the low end. It contained fishing equipment in one of the drawers that lined the waterline. Drawers held stereo music, pc with internet connection (not that I wanted it), movie satellite, freezer, storage for food and a fold out bed. Life would be simple. I could drift along with the ocean current, pull into a harbor anytime and tie up, or jump off for a daily swim. My dream house.

My dream plan, become a Great Looper. Never stay put ever again.

Once I motored out to the gulf current, I soon forgot my exposure to the world, even embraced nakedness. What did I need with life so simple? I became one with the sea and its plants and the creatures that lived around me. Most of the time, they were my sole companions.

My nature tended toward lovey-dovey take care of everyone syndrome. True nannyhood, absolute momism exemplified my life until then. Not that old habits weren't hard to break.

I wore my usual neck-to-foot-flannel nightgown to bed the first night. I don't remember how long it took to realize clothes didn't matter.

My daily habit was to wake naturally—I sealed the living chamber and sank down a good hundred feet to get that good dark feeling of nighttime while I slept. When I woke, I'd rise up, take my bearings—test the water temperature, looked for bubbles racing north, and my GPS against the sea charts on my computer. I'd type up my location and any thoughts that came to mind. Then I'd open up the solar lounge and climb down to the paddleboat attachment and get a good five miles up the current. It increased my chances of meeting new people and creatures and kept me fit and limber. At any sign of vehicles out and about—fishing boats, coast guard, ships loaded with container, sure, I'd put on a robe, just because I know how people get with binoculars. Yes, I used mine too. Then I'd scoop up any small fish near my home, cutting them up to prime my crab and shrimp pots.

Sometimes I'd swim or snorkel. Sometimes I'd lie in the lounger and watch the waves break far off on the beach, usually on overcast days, although I had a sun umbrella here, too. Sometimes I'd have spare bait I could throw out to attract a crowd of pelagic birds.

Prime time of day was watching the kill.

Oh, right. I'm not supposed to admit to that thrill. Was it a deep longing for death, allowing me to join my departed husband? Depression and loneliness? Lack of contact with other people?

Well, no. None of those. Not that I consciously think about it.

Perhaps it's living under a daily death threat that does it.

Ha ha. Now you are probably thinking, she's gone nutso or

is exaggerating the danger. Truly, I never thought of myself as likely to die.

Every week, up until I reached the St. Lawrence River delta, I pulled into small-town harbors and bought supplies. I found reasons to chat with people. I delayed waitresses to chat while I slowly savored steak and baked potato. Mail people, grocery store clerks, doctors, they all were good practice for my voice. Music clerks too, since I signed up and began taking opera lessons. Bread, eggs, butter, freezer goods: vegetables, meat I kept stocked up, just in case of mishap. I tended toward vegetarianism.

On one of these trips, I paired up with Lewis for a time. Lewis dressed high-class mariner, collar, deck shoes, captain's hat, the whole bit. You wouldn't think him the type to get his hands bloody. But turn him out, give him a hard-deck inflatable with trolling motor, bait him up for Bluefin, underneath the fine scent of musk his muscles showed bench press quality definition. He taught me about the strike. The play, the long demanding hours of reeling one in.

He toted the sharpest knife north of Jacksonville: pry out shellfish in seconds, filet a fish in not much more. The sweet salty taste of red meat, rolled on the tongue, silky sliminess of oyster dropping down throat, touch of lemon to chase it made our companionship over merlot too tasty.

Our relation turned ugly after I tired of endless sushi and vino hangovers. I didn't want commitment. His kind better suited a mental hospital. I snuck into town, got a tow by a cruiser, and thank heavens didn't see him again.

However, just to make sure, I backtracked to see if anyone followed. A waitress passed on the news. Lewis had taken up with a thirty-something bleach job. The next months passed in lonely contemplation of my friends, the pelagic birds. At first I'd only thrown out chum once a day.

I admit it. The sticky smell of blood turned me on. It didn't take long before the albatross soared in, dipping their broad wings ever so slightly before plopping down. The stabbing dive of the gannet. The squabble of the laughing gulls. Why? I guess when death reaches out to you, you either give in, just do away with yourself or feast on life. Ha ha. Just between you and me, I tasted the chum. A little salty, intensely fishy, sticky even on your tongue. I got so obsessed with feeding them I sometimes chummed three or four times a day.

All was great. I was nearing the entrance to the St. Lawrence Seaway one day when I woke up. There he was, a great white shark staring me eyeball to eyeball. I couldn't move. Couldn't think. When I finally caved to the need to pee, he bonked my home. Gulp.

I slid down to the floor, wiped up my mess with an old towel, slithered back to bed. I risked another bonk to get crackers. This went on for days. I couldn't rise up to the surface; he might dine on me for breakfast. I couldn't move around my home. I had to wear clothing. I shiver to think of those steel green eyes, those horridly sharp teeth. I could even smell the stench of rotting fish on him. This was it, my death, not slowly falling to sleep, but a sharp crunch, myself horridly screaming before final blessed black emptiness.

Then he went away. Still I didn't move. I couldn't. The next day I puttered into the river, clouds building off the north. I knew it meant storm, horrible storm. I should have tied up at a dock, checked into a motel. But after senor shark, I finally had enough of sea, death, blood, nasty biting, grabbing birds. I wanted the rain to cleanse me free, to live.

Even with a weighted keel, fishbowl shaped homes and storms don't go together. Like a hamster in a ball, I crashed and churned and scrambled and puked through 10 days of nasty life and when the storm ended, I was further north than I intended. When I rode the Ohio and Mississippi down south, I went with the storm surge, dodging huge floating trees and paddling full out even as I motored. One half year before the mast seduced, badgered, bruted and scrambled me back to life. I was thankful for every drop of rain that cleansed me free of myself. I was free of my grief, ready to take on love, travel the world, taste the finer things in life.

What I got was dear old Rubio Hernan. I was willing to deal, just as long as he took this dratted floating home off my hands. I gave him a call. He showed up one night.

He slipped aboard after midnight. I vaguely heard the splash. The creak as someone descended the stairs. Next thing I knew, he had a knife at my throat.

But that nasty white shark had taught me a thing or two. I kept a shark prod beside my bed. Gave him a good zap. With Rubio out, I checked his wallet. I was more than mad enough to call the police in, but not sure I wanted to badly enough to be stuck with the fishbowl.

Imagine. Fifty grand in his wallet. That was good enough for me even if I lost half I put in. I signed over the deed, called it an even trade.

Before I left, I zapped him in each foot just to be sure he understood where he stood when he woke up.

Dear old Rubio cured me of the fishbowl, but not of feeding chum to the gulls. Ha ha.

About the Author:

Sheri loves to travel the world, make a splash, and find unusual ways to speculate about the future in poetry and prose. In a former life she worked in Aviation computing. She currently lives in Orlando, FL.

Sheri Harper: sherifresonkeharper.com, http://about.me/sfharper, http://xeeme.com/sfharper, Freelance Travel, Technology and Science Writer, Chimera # 6 New World Disorder, Tales of the Talisman, Beacons of Tomorrow, No Stone Unturned

The New Pirates

by Catherine A. Callaghan

Bill Martin was about to mail his latest article, "Insights on Relative Clauses," to *Linguistic Investigations* when an inner urge compelled him to check his mailbox first. Under a notice from the Belleporte Chapter of the American Professors Association and an appeal from Save-the-Snails Foundation, he found the first issue of a new journal from India, *Eastern Linguistics*, with a book mark. He flipped to the page in question and froze. The article was entitled "New Light on Old Clauses," and the first paragraph looked identical to the manuscript he was about to mail off.

He sat down hard and reopened his manuscript to check more carefully. The second paragraph of the Indian article was also identical, the third and fourth differed by a few words, and the conclusions were stated differently. The article looked like an earlier version of his manuscript which he'd presented to the Linguistic Association of America a few years previously. Kyle Townsend, assistant professor at Harvard University, claimed authorship, a name Bill failed to recognize.

"God damn it," he said to the empty office. "This is my reward for sharing my research. I should have kept it to myself."

Belleporte was an East Coast city with a rich history dating from early Colonial times. Twenty miles to the north, there was an inlet called "Pirate's Cove" where 17th century buccaneers had once threatened East Coast shipping, but their influence waned after a hurricane destroyed their vessel. There was more than one form of piracy, however.

It was now 1990. Bill would soon come up for tenure review in the Language Science Department at Belleporte University. His colleagues hinted that they wanted him to chair the department, and he needed full credit for this article. Gone were the days when professors of linguistics were so rare they were hired before completing their dissertations and given automatic tenure if they showed promise. Now requirements in many university departments were high enough that some Nobel Prize laureates would have failed to meet them in their day. Self-plagiarism was one way a desperate assistant professor could pad his resume; that is, by publishing the same article under different titles in two different countries. Plagiarism of another professor's work was rare, but it did occur as it had in this case.

Bill considered his options. He could report Townsend to the ethics committee of the Linguistic Association of America, but that process was painful and time-consuming, especially since he'd discarded all earlier drafts of his article once he'd completed the final version. The easiest thing was to devote all his energy to writing a related article and hope he could finish it in time for his tenure review.

He wondered if Townsend had cited him at all. He found only a casual reference: "At the 1986 LAA annual meeting, William Martin presented a superficial summary of the problems discussed here." He felt slow fury rise—1986 was the year the LAA had met at Harvard, the year he'd presented the paper Townsend had plagiarized. Townsend's treatment of him was especially unfair since he'd always gone out of his way to acknowledge the contributions of others, often to the point of embarrassment. A graduate assistant had once complained, "You needn't have given me credit for drawing boundary lines on your diagrams."

He returned to the question of who had left the new journal in his mailbox. He examined the bookmark. It was cream-colored with the official Belleporte logo, an old-fashioned gate emblazoned with a bat plus the slogan "Portal to the Past, Gateway to the Future." The bat symbolized Belleporte's association with vampires, which the Chamber of Commerce exploited to attract tourists, a connection that embarrassed some intellectuals at the university. These bookmarks were available throughout the city and gave no clue as to the owner's identity.

Bill then considered each of his colleagues in turn. Stephanie Jones was acting chair of the Language Science Department, and she would have confronted him in person if she'd discovered Townsend's article. Sally Foster, a dialect specialist, was friendly and open, and she would have left a note, as would Myra Holmes and newly hired John Hollister. Computer expert Jacob Bloom was more secretive, but Bill couldn't imagine him acquiring expertise on theoretical linguistic issues in India. Too bad he'd failed to share his earlier draft with any of them—

"Quite a puzzle, isn't it?"

Bill almost jumped a foot, even though he was still seated. He was facing the west window of the department office. The sun had set and the sky was aflame with red clouds. He turned around. A well-dressed man of slight build had entered so quietly that Bill hadn't noticed him. His clothing was entirely black and seemed to date from an earlier period in history. Bill knew he'd seen the gentleman before, but he couldn't recall where.

"You were kind enough to give me a ride a few years back, remember? My name is Mack," replied the visitor, as if reading Bill's mind.

Martin had a hazy recollection of the encounter during his student days at Ohio State University when he'd worked as a truck driver on the Belleporte run. He struggled to recall the details, but was unable to do so, remembering only that they were unpleasant. He felt no desire to tangle with Mack again.

"What do you want?" he asked.

"I thought we might be of mutual assistance to each other again. It's shameful the way some academics will stop at nothing to inflate their accomplishments, don't you think?"

Bill said nothing, since he doubted Mack cared one way or the other. "Why did you leave that journal in my mailbox?" he finally asked.

"With your high level of integrity, Bill, I knew you wouldn't want to submit an article if its authorship was clouded."

Bill was already upset, and it took all his willpower to refrain from attacking Mack. Townsend's stolen article was in a new journal from India that he doubted anyone at Belleporte had heard about. If Mack hadn't alerted him, he could have submitted his own article to *Linguistic Investigations* as he had planned. The chances are no one would have been the wiser, except Townsend. If someone did notice, Bill could have pled ignorance. Now that avenue was closed.

"Because of you, I may not be granted tenure. I'll have to leave Belleporte at the end of the next academic year, but I think you already know that. If Belleporte University denies me tenure, other universities won't want to hire me. Get out of here, dammit!" he finally said.

"What? Before you've heard my plan?"

Bill struggled again to recall details of his last encounter with Mack, but they still eluded him. He wanted no part of anything Mack might propose, but after looking into the stranger's intense green eyes, he decided to hear the man out.

"I work for Mrs. Isobel Bode, and she must have an immediate search on the title of a piece of real estate that interests her. The Wolf County Office is open between 9 a.m. and 4 p.m. tomorrow. I'd go myself, but I'm otherwise engaged during those hours. I'd appreciate it if you did the search for me."

"Mrs. Bode is the richest woman in Belleporte," said Bill. "Her lawyers could do the job better than I could."

"They're too well-known, I'm afraid. Secrecy is of the essence in this case because Mrs. Bode wants to make her offer for the land before the owner has a chance to raise the price. Besides, I'd hate to report to her that you'd been uncooperative."

Bill felt as if he was sliding from the frying pan into the fire. Mrs. Bode was notorious in her business dealings for skirting the boundaries of the law, meaning her enemies would be watching for any misstep. He had no desire to become an accessory to an illegal transaction if the matter should go to court. But she was also a campus benefactor, and he couldn't risk making her an enemy so he reluctantly agreed to the arrangement.

"Meet me here tomorrow night after sunset," said Mack, "and bring me a full written report."

Bill was about to ask what he'd receive in return, but when he looked around, Mack was gone, and he'd taken the Indian journal with him. He'd left so quietly that Bill hadn't heard the door click shut. He examined the door carefully. It fit tightly into its frame with a space underneath through which students often submitted overdue assignments. He checked the outside knob and froze again. It locked automatically when the door closed. The mystery was not how Mack had left the office without making a sound. It was how he'd entered through a locked door in the first place.

The red clouds had darkened and the western horizon was turning green when Bill left the L & L building and walked toward his car. Forsythia flamed against a fence under the knotted limbs of an old maple tree. Soon the dogwood would bloom, followed by purple knots on the redbud. Dandelions poked through manicured lawns, much to the embarrassment of campus gardeners, but Bill always liked them. They were considered weeds only because they were persistent. If they'd been hard to grow, they'd be considered beautiful treasures.

Bill passed the Percival Sloane Dining Hall that honored a famous Belleportite from Colonial times. Patriotic citizens often compared Sloane with Benjamin Franklin. Indeed, both men had owned printing presses and had worked their way to the top of their enterprises, but there the resemblance ended. Sloane had used his press to crank out Continental currency during the Revolutionary War and became wealthy through dubious land transactions. Bill had cynically assumed that such activities were overlooked because Sloane had donated a portion of his estate to establish Belleporte University, but townspeople who had no connection with the campus also celebrated Sloan. There was a more important reason—success! Like Franklin, Sloane had been successful in his operations. It was no coincidence that Mrs. Bode was one of Sloan's admirers.

By the time Bill reached his car, the green of the western sky had faded to a black backdrop with cold white stars. Chill air mingled with the scent of honeysuckle, symbolizing the battle of the seasons that took place every spring as winter hung on into late April before it relinquished its bite. He wished he'd brought his jacket.

That night, Bill tossed and turned. Mack had provided no solution to his own problem. He started composing a new article on relative clauses, but his heart wasn't in it. He might finish it in time for his review, and it would probably be enough to qualify him for tenure, but he'd already written a definitive article with major implications that should establish his reputation as a theoretical linguist. He thought again of Townsend's slight in addition to his piracy. For some reason that slight stung more than the plagiarism itself.

"If my treatment was superficial," he asked out loud, "why did Townsend steal my article?" Bill decided to fight back even if it meant risking tenure. There was no way he'd let that son of a bitch take the credit that belonged to him. He resolved to telephone colleagues he knew well and write the rest in hopes of recovering a dated copy of his 1986 paper to present to his tenure committee along with his current version that he'd almost mailed off.

Finally, he drifted into a fitful sleep. He awoke the next morning to a milky-gray sky that mirrored his mood, and he barely had time to gather the papers for his nine o'clock class. His office hour followed along with three students who had time-consuming problems. Since he was pressed for time, he considered ignoring his promise to Mack, but decided against it. He'd given his word, which still meant something in Colonial Belleporte, even if it was ignored elsewhere. Bill skipped lunch in order to conduct the title search in the county office, prudently allowing twice the time he thought would be necessary. He finished shortly before the office closed for the day. Typing his report took all the time remaining before his evening appointment. He arrived at the department office the same time as Mack.

"The title seems clear," Bill reported, "but legal terminology isn't my specialty."

Mack studied the report and announced that Bill was right. "It's a good thing you agreed to do the search, or Mrs. Bode would have been forced to acquire the adjacent property, which happens to be where your house is located."

Bill shivered even though it was a warm evening. Deciphering legal phrases had so engrossed him that afternoon that he'd paid no attention to the location of the property in question. His mortgage was with the Bank of Belleporte, another of Isobel Bode's holdings, and he'd been overdue on a few payments. He had no doubt she could find grounds for foreclosure and eviction if she wanted. Vacating his house at the present time would be impossible since he knew of no other house he could move into.

"By the way," said Mack, "you can feel free to submit your article to *Linguistic Investigations* as you'd planned. Harvard keeps a file of all papers presented to the Linguistic Association of America even if you don't. I sent my copy of the Indian journal along with an explanatory letter to Townsend's chairman. I doubt your friend, Kyle, will remain at Harvard for long."

With these words, Mack transformed into a white mist and oozed under the door. Suddenly the details of Bill's last encounter with Mack resurfaced. The gentleman was a vampire with great powers at night, including the knack of charming others into doing his will and the ability to assume etheric form and pass through tight places. But he was helpless during the day.

In the 1950s, the Belleporte Chamber of Commerce had debated how to promote tourism to bring much-needed money to the city. The choice for an official Belleporte theme had been between pirates who'd only briefly threatened East Coast shipping and vampires who continued to surface in eye-witness accounts, despite the skepticism of the well-educated. After much discussion, the vampires won out. Better successful vampires than unsuccessful buccaneers.

About the Author:

Catherine A. Callaghan writes speculative fiction that skirts the boundary between the real and the unreal. "Night Run," also set in Belleporte, appeared in LocoThology 2012. In her other life, she is a semi-retired professor of linguistics specializing in Central California Indian languages.

Alongside the Coastline of Sumatra . . .

by Sergio 'ente per ente' Palumbo

"Land is the secure ground of home,
the sea is like life, the outside, the unknown . . ."
by Stephen Gardiner

The sailing ship that passed through that perilous stretch of sea, over the past few years, was known by many names, but the most common was, *The Vessel of the Possessed.* The majority of people thought it only a legend or hearsay filled with fancy, tall tales seamen entrusted to each other in low tones while in ill-reputed taverns late at night—especially when they were drunk and visibly hyped-up. And what they said was true.

The whole crew of the pirate junk named *Uxia* was well aware of it. In fact, that cursed sailing ship now stood just beyond the bow, only a few leagues away. Its sturdy hull was a dark chestnut, the sails spread out between two tall masts, allowing for a powerful surface, and the standing rigging was mainly absent.

Captain Roberto leaned over his *Beladau's* sheath—a short curved dagger from Borneo, very keen and with a convex cutting edge that he himself had pulled out of the corpse of his opponent more than ten years ago. His black hair was disheveled over wide shoulders, and he was wrapped in his usual whitish short-sleeved shirt. Captain Roberto stood still, looking toward the front without saying a single word.

The fifty-seven-years-old Portuguese seafarer had a proud look on a face that was shriveled because of the saltiness of the air. His cold eyes stood out. He had long stopped doubting the ship's existence, as this certainly wasn't the first time he had crossed its path on the high seas.

The first appearance happened one year prior. He and his crewmembers had been along the coastline of Sumatra. They had just ended an attack against one of the many small villages crammed with damp hovels. Such places were poorly fortified, allowing Roberto to seize their possessions and kill any government soldiers who stumbled into their path.

Up to that day the Portuguese captain had lost hope of ever finding his son again, who was a pirate like himself, although 17 years younger. He hadn't heard from him since leaving to lead an incursion past Weh Island. Roberto was afraid his son might have been chased down and killed by some well-armed *lancang* of the government.

In fact he knew that over the course of those summer months in 1628, Muda, the ruler of the strong Sultanate of Aceh, had started a concerted hunt for the pirates that continuously assaulted and plundered the coasts of his realm, by deploying all of his military sailing ships to guard most of the area. The seafarer wasn't sure his son had really been killed during a fight, of course, but he well knew him. Although not too accustomed to thinking for long, and surely endowed with a hot temper, he didn't think his son's ship had sunk simply because of a sudden storm. More than likely government troops had captured him and put him to death, maybe by pouncing on him with a preponderance of forces.

This was why Roberto had decided he was going to pay them back for what their ruler had done, by devastating everything around. At this moment he and his men had ravaged five coastal villages by seizing all the useful supplies in the area and killing, by the sword, all the inhabitants they'd met ashore.

The event with the *Vessel of the Possessed* occurred the day of their last raid in that zone. Captain Roberto's huge, though fast, junk had been at full sail, moving away from the coastline and heading for the open sea, when the wind suddenly dropped and didn't blow for the rest of the evening. After some hours of tiresome immobility, he thought about employing all of his crewmembers to man the oars, if necessary. That way they might finally edge away from that damn stretch of sea and move to safer waters, shielded from the fast military lancangs of the government. Anyway, before he could put his plan into action, that incredible thing happened, and it changed his life for sure.

While the seafarers looked warily at one another, the lookout—a young hairless Indonesian guy who was bolt upright at the maintop at the head of the mainmast—signaled that a distant sail had come into view. Fear started pervading the crewmembers. While they were asking themselves if it was one of the many well-armed lancangs of Muda—usually filled with more than 400 soldiers—or only a common merchant vessel, somebody pointed out that it seemed really strange that the ship moved so quickly across the water, especially given that there were no oarsmen alongside, and the wind hadn't started blowing again. Despite all of that, the full surface of sails was clearly inflated and billowing off the wooden hull without a problem.

The air of mystery slowly turned to alarm among the crew. Then someone supposed it might only be a natural event. Maybe the wind was blowing only at that point, while it was completely still in the area their junk was stopped in. On the other hand, several men thought it was an unnatural, inexplicable situation. In the end, an old seaman revealed his hidden fear. The ship was the famous *Vessel of the Possessed:* There was no real doubt about it, and that was why it could magically move without being affected by the dead calm.

"The Vessel of the Possessed"!

That piece of gossip spread among the seamen as fast as the morning mist that covered the forested shores of Belitung, which was usually enveloped in a thick humid fog for most of the early morning hours each day. Whatever the truth, they were unable to do a single thing to quickly move away.

The captain was well aware of their situation. Moreover, maybe they had no time to come to speed or change their course, even though gusts of wind were blowing out to deeper sea, in favor of their ship, as that unknown vessel's course suggested.

Maybe it really was possessed, explaining why it came on at such a considerable speed.

On the long crowded deck, made up of softwoods, some unending minutes of apprehension passed. Fear was reflected on the darkened and anxious faces of every single crewmember, until the approaching ship drew within a few hundred yards. Although usually hard-nosed, bloody and familiar with battles, most of those seamen gave in to their secret fears when facing unearthly things. They probably would have even dove into the water, in order to find an immediate escape, provided they hadn't known that the water in the area was full of terrible blue sharks. Soon, the men aboard were looking at the opposite deck, and they closely stared at the whole expanse of that cursed two-masted vessel.

It was a big surprise to discover that there were some real-live seamen busy maneuvering that unknown hull, seamen just like them. Those were moments of trepidation while that ship sailed nearer and nearer the *Uxia*. It came within five yards, going by very fast, without any of the other crew seeming to even notice their junk. It passed in the complete silence, at times interrupted only by wheezes or breaths from the pirates.

The unknown sailing ship swayed with the waves, while inexorably proceeding along. It was more or less the same size as their junk, incredibly emitting only a continuous sound of crackling boards. It was in just that moment that Captain Roberto, by looking at that cursed vessel's upper deck, became sure that he noticed some familiar features. He didn't believe his own eyes as he grabbed the spyglass in order to verify his vision. One of those strange crewmembers very closely resembled his missing son. The man in his glass had the same dark pupils, long hair and wide shirt he'd previously worn while leading raids of plunder onto the shoreline. But also some of the seamen next to his son reminded Roberto of other known faces. Many of them resembled the crewmembers the young man had brought with him during his last voyage.

Roberto would have reached him and made sure of all that in person, moved his motionless junk along by means of his own arms, even jumped on it if possible, but there was nothing he could do. This made him feel powerless, weak, unable to discover the truth that seemed finally ahead of him.

He cried out again and again, *"Son, son! I'm your father. Answer me. Look at me over here, on this side,"* while leaning over the wooden bulwark so far that he almost fell overboard.

There came no reply.

The unknown vessel dispersed away, proceeding at the same unnatural rate it had approached. It disappeared in the distance, as if it had never really existed or had been a mirage, to the astonishment of the whole crew.

The wind finally came back for the *Uxia* late that night, and at last the pirates were able to head for the high sea. But the Portuguese seafarer remained restless for the rest of the trip.

* * * * *

From that day on everything changed for Captain Roberto. He began to collect information about the so-called *"Vessel of the Possessed"* at every seaport. He queried the owners of every tavern he knew, collecting all the hearsay statements about that ship that were being passed around by other pirates.

A lot of people had already heard about the vessel. According to a few local seamen, it had a crew of cursed individuals, hated by all the gods. Other people thought they were dead sailors doomed to forever chase their plunder, having forgotten where they had hidden it while still in the world of the living. But there were even more incredible opinions, certainly figments of imaginations coming out of too many glasses of bad wine.

It took several months for him, but in the end the Portuguese captain found a useful clue: among all the alleged sightings, there was one that occurred three times, on different dates, next to Tanahbala Island. And those were testimonials coming from men he knew personally—trustworthy people he frequently hobnobbed with.

So, that ship had crossed those waters many times. Maybe it was part of its usual course, whatever that might prove to be. From that point on, he had to begin in earnest, if he ever wanted to see his son again!

And a new encounter over that seemingly unending expanse did occur soon. *But things went in a very different way than he expected.*

* * * * *

Now that the vessel was before Roberto's eyes again he thought it certainly couldn't escape! And his son was still on that deck. He had already seen him while looking at the ship from afar.

"Ready on my mark, *damn rabble!*" the captain exclaimed. He lowered his hand and ordered the attack.

There was a wild clamor while the pirates armed themselves and got ready to board the ship. That sea craft was damned fast, so the captain ordered his crew to put on more sails in order to ensure their junk reached the other ship after chasing it in the open sea. They would board as soon as the opportunity presented itself, sooner or later. Finally, the new powerful sails were flawlessly shoving the *Uxia* over the waves towards that decisive encounter.

His present crew was very different from the one onboard the first time Roberto chanced upon the *Vessel of the Possessed*. It hadn't been easy to find men eager to follow him and to put aside their deep superstitions. After conveniently defoliating the rabble of all the weak ones—just as you might prune all the dead branches out a tree so it looked better in your garden—it had proven necessary to include and mingle the new group he had personally chosen with the remaining previous crewmembers. Of course, in order to adequately motivate the sailors to do what was needed, the captain had been forced to tell them that a lot of riches and valuables were onboard that unknown ship—which represented the only real objective of his—enough, in fact, that it would easily allow everyone to finally live a safe, wealthy existence forever.

Roberto unsheathed his *Beladau,* while clasping the wheel-lock in his left hand. The weapon was the one he always wore at his waist, along with the yellowish worn-out trousers. This was the kind of gun used since 1550, so-called because a rotating steel wheel provided ignition. It was very reliable because it had a better resistance to damp conditions than other firearms and didn't emit a telltale glow. This, however, proved to be a danger while in proximity to gunpowder, when dealing with other more modern pistols.

The pirates menacingly moved onwards to the deck of their prey, over the sloshing waves that wallowed under their feet, climbing down just like a throng of starving wild beasts past the wooden bulwark. An eddy of pointed metallic barongs, war-axes, swords and a few lonely shots followed. Coarse cries filled the air all around, adding to the din of the confused assault.

As soon as the captain arrived at the upper deck, he found himself before a middle-aged man who didn't even try to protect his own body. The captain's pistol shot him in the middle of the chest, making the man collapse to the dusty boards. Roberto went on, towards the quarter-deck where he had just glimpsed his son's figure.

When he was finally able to directly look at him, his son was busy giving orders to the other crewmembers of that cursed ship. Roberto's heart beat fast.

The young man turned to him and stared in silence. From the glimmer he saw in his son's eyes, Roberto considered that maybe he had finally noticed and recognized his father.

But the man looked to be speechless now, so it was the older Portuguese's who turned to speak. "Helder!" he cried out. "You're my son, Helder, aren't you?"

The young man remained for some time more in silence then his mouth opened in a sneering tone: "The body I occupy at present recognizes your appearance. You're the pirate called

Roberto, the captain of the *Uxia*! And I'm your son, or better, I was him."

The old seafarer felt amazed because of that unexpected, strange answer. He quickly formed a reply. Then he considered his words and asked, "What do you mean? You still are my son, aren't you?"

"Regardless of the person your son was before, everything changed the day his sailing ship reached Onbekend Island. He stumbled into us," the one replied.

"You . . . *who*? Tell me now, who are you? What did you do to my son and to his ship? Speak at once or I'll pierce your chest by means of my sword!"

"We're *Badi!*" the young man—or the creature that seemed to be so—stated.

Badi! They were those legendary beings who the seamen had talked about for a very long time. Roberto would have never truly believed such a thing could turn out to be real, until today. Dead creatures—coming out just from the worst fairy tales and old sea myths—that could take possession of the bodies of men, even of objects. They were feared in the most secluded villages onshore, as well!

While the captain had a difficult time trying to recover from that last terrible statement, the thing that stood just before him began his tale. "All of us, long ago, belonged to a pirate crew just like yours, being always bloody and hungry for riches. We preyed on merchant ships and villages alongside the coastline of Sumatra, leaving nothing more behind us than death and destruction.

But one day, one among us, a missionary who long ago had turned to evil, ending up losing himself and becoming a restless plunderer, had another change of heart. He decided he would do all he could in order to prevent the whole population of a small village from being killed by our most brazen crewmembers. This was because he had handled some religious activities there in the past. They were all going to be killed because their chief didn't want to reveal where he had hidden the gold that had previously adorned a local temple.

Anyway, as he was unable to convince everyone to simply turn around and leave, he thought it would be better to scupper our vessel so the attention of everyone was temporarily diverted. The inhabitants escaped our grip in the end. But he was discovered and tortured for a very long time. He finally died at the break of dawn. His devastated corpse was left on a hidden shore of the lost island of Onbekend, where we stopped for only one night on the way back from that stretch of sea." A brief pause followed his words. "Moreover, the ex-missionary, before dying, vehemently cursed. In fact our ship became beached not too far from that island and was soon destroyed because of the strong waves, making the crew swim ashore and hide on Onbekend.

Over the course of the next few weeks we were easily able to survive, thanks to the provisions taken away from our lost vessel, by drinking the water from a small spring on the island, and hunting the local game. But all of that lasted for a very short time. Finally there was nothing left, and hunger began mastering our minds and wills. I, the captain, was one of the last. Nonetheless, death came for me the same as it did for all the others, among no inconsiderable wrenching pains."

Captain Roberto listened to that tale, enchanted in a way, uncertain about what to do exactly, his pistol still in his left hand ready to shoot. "And what about my son? Why did you seize his body? What did he ever do to you?"

"Helder's sailing ship and his crew came to that island early in the evening, on the anniversary of when we died 30 years before. He was trying to escape from a warlike government lancang that had already captured his junk while his sailors were drunk in a small port's tavern. After the seizer, he hurriedly boarded another vessel, along with the remains of his crew. He had been forced to steal that one and put to sea. That is this ship. But the other lancang ceaselessly followed him for many weeks.

When he made it to our island and stumbled onto our bony remains scattered on the shore, it was a very good opportunity for our restless and wandering souls. We couldn't miss the chance. We knew we had to take it immediately! And so we seized their bodies in order to again become capable of maneuvering a ship, escaping forever that lost place in the sea. Finally we could return to earth, even though beneath different human faces."

The eyes of the Portuguese pirate shuddered in anger. He clasped the fire weapon with fury and aimed it at the young man's head, almost unable to reason any further.

"You can't hit me, pirate! Otherwise you'll damage the body of your own son."

That stopped Roberto at once. Then, after turning to look at the heap of corpses on the wooden boards of the upper deck below, he said, "Your men have already deprived our vessel of too many of our sailors. If just a few more of the bodies we presently occupy die over the course of the battle we could be unable to maneuver this ship and we'd really be lost forever. *Give Helder back to me!* Leave his body now!" the pirate ordered.

"Believe me, that's exactly what I would like to do. As a matter of fact, all of us only wanted to make use of the bodies of the crewmembers to get to the mainland and simply move into other, better bodies. But we can't do it, the same as we can't get off this ship or stop our endless seafaring."

"Why? How come?"

"Because of the evil curse affecting us all. In fact, as soon as we got aboard and started moving away from Onbekend Island, the soul of that dead priest seized a living body, the one of a powerful creature of the sea, a giant Fe'e, more precisely!

"What are you saying? A Fe'e? It's just a monstrous legendary creature, nothing more—"

"And yet it exists, and that possessed beast chases all of us, hiding in the depths of this ocean ever since the day we boarded this vessel, making us run away continuously, in order to hang on. We can feel its presence, the worrisome vigil that it keeps, its closeness to our hull, even though it never shows itself over the surface before mortal eyes. It is slow, yet indefatigable, and only by using our cursed Badi powers can we hold it back and sail our ship faster than seems possible. But if we ever stop, it would soon reach us and destroy this ship along with all the seamen onboard, leaving us *Badi* to forever wander the sea, the same as all the dead men who were never buried in the ground."

At that point, Captain Roberto hesitated. "What can I do, then? I won't let my son remain the prey of your kind, damned creatures!"

"There's another way."

"What is that?"

"This sailing ship needs an expert captain, and you are an expert captain, indeed. If you just let me seize your body, then I'll be able to finally release your son. He will be allowed to board your junk, along with the rest of your crew, and return to land." A brief silence followed. "What do you decide, then?"

"What can I do in order to make this happen? Why should I trust you?"

"It's very easy, all I need to do is stretch out my hand and touch you. This way my soul will pass from this body to yours and your son, Helder, will be free again. It will only take one motion."

"*Only one motion . . . .*" Roberto considered.

"Only a motion like this," the *Badi* repeated, in a persuasive voice, slowly approaching and reaching the old seafarer. His fingers touched him.

Then everything was accomplished. The Portuguese captain didn't even find the time to welcome his son back to consciousness, as the *Badi* had completely taken possession of him.

Roberto turned to his crewmembers, who were still fighting on the upper deck, and simply told them. "Stop the battle! We have reached an agreement."

* * * * *

The vessel that was going across that stretch of sea was well known to the seafarers. It had many names, the most common of which was, for sure, *The Vessel of the Possessed*. A lot of people considered it only one of those legends sailors told each other in low tones while staying in old taverns late at night, especially when alcohol seized their minds.

And yet what the legends said was true. Helder, the new captain of the junk called *Uxia* was well aware of all that. He was very proud to have this ship at his service, as the lower, sturdy part was made of three decks, which made it better to resist the storms which occurred frequently around there. In a way, the *Uxia* was much better than any other vessel he had ever owned before, for sure, but there wasn't time to take pleasure from that. Some serious matter lay just ahead of him at present.

He leaned to the sheath of his long *Beladau*—the weapon that had once been his father's. Long black hair around his face, the young seafarer looked ahead of him, without speaking. He knew that his father, Captain Roberto, was still on that damned cursed vessel, the one who had let him gain his freedom again one year ago, because of an agreement made with the chief of those terrible creatures, the *Badi*. It was they who ruled over that ship, always on the run to escape the sea monster who pursued them night and day in order to make them pay for their faults and crimes. And yet, thanks to that agreement, his father had taken his place at the lead of that ship. Since then, Helder had intended to find a way to finally free himself, at any cost!

On that vessel there was also his previous crew, or the men that were still left of it, a double reason to keep faith with his obligation.

It had cost him a lot of money, and a long time too, before finding a safe way to forever free those seamen possessed by the cruel restless *Badi*. But, thanks to an old shaman from a lonely coastal village, he had been able to trace all the ingredients, the ritual itself and the formulary capable of definitely casting all those evil beings from the living. All that he needed was leaves, along with a few shrubs called *pulut-pulut* and *selaguri*, mingled with some small branches of *gandarusa* and *lenjuang merah*, wrapped in a big leaf of dry *si-pulih* and held together by means of a piece of tree bark. Everything had to be put into a bucket of fresh water, and then the beverage made out of all those things had to be drunk by those men while the shaman completed the ritual, pronouncing the required words.

Today he would put an end to their unholy existence and free his father, along with all the other crewmembers aboard that damn vessel. Hopefully, *forever*.

About the Author:

Sergio (nickname: 'ente per ente') is an Italian public servant who graduated from Law School, working in the public real estate branch. He published a Fantasy RolePlaying illustrated Manual, WarBlades, of more than 700 pages. He likes to write both in Italian and English, and some of his works in American/English have been published on American Aphelion Webzine, WeirdYear Webzine, YesterYearFiction, AnotheRealm Magazine, Alien Skin Magazine, on Orion's Child Science Fiction and Fantasy Magazine, Farther Stars Than These, on Digital Dragon Magazine, on Kalkion Science Fiction and Fantasy Web Magazine, on Quantum Muse, Surprising Stories, on EMG-ZINE, on The Speculative Edge Magazine, on Australian Antipodean SF, on British Schlock! Webzine, on Australian SQ Mag and in print inside 4 British Sci-Fi/Horror Anthology, 6 American Fantasy/Horror/Urban Fantasy Anthologies and 1 Australian Sci-Fi Anthology so far, and 12 more to come by various publishers in 2013 and 2014. He is also a scale modeler who likes mostly Science Fiction/Fantasy and Real Space models and writes articles/reportages about his works or about some scale model shows'.

This is internet site of his Model Club "La Centuria": www.lacenturia.it

The Weight of Treasure

by Bear Weiter

The man sat on a bench overlooking the ocean, watching everything but the endless waves. He abhorred the picturesque seascape, the vast horizon and the promise of the black depths below it. Still, he sat, day after day.

Occasionally someone passed by—couples walking hand-in-hand, or the solo runner. They kept to their own, never nodding, never waving, and he did the same.

Each afternoon, though, a boy emerged from down the coast. No more than eight or nine, he wore a black pirate hat and carried a wooden sword. An eye patch stretched across his face, tilted up above his right eye so he could see out of both. The boy ran along the sand, slashing and cursing at imaginary foes. He did this with a big toothy grin on his face, a near-perfect example of simple happiness.

The man envied this boy. He longed for days full of carefree play, of no worries or stress, of no commitments or guilt. He found no irony in this—coming to this beach each day, and still wanting what it should have provided. No, this was his prison, a place he had no choice but to visit again and again, no other option but to dwell on his thoughts, as weighed down by his past as he was with the large duffle bag he carried.

As a corporate consultant—a corporate raider, really—he had destroyed more lives than he could count. Some called it greed, but to him it had been merely day-to-day activities, a Darwinian approach to business that forced rapid evolution or instantaneous extinction. For himself, what he touched turned to gold; for others, not so much.

This irony—of watching a boy play pirate, while he had

essentially been one—was not lost on him.

He did not wish to think about his former life—it had never bothered him before—but after the accident he could no longer ignore the personal costs of his actions. The body count, both figuratively and literally, had become too much of a burden. Now, he could no longer think of anything else. Like coming here to this beach when he wanted to be far, far away, his mind refused any thoughts of peace. His will was not his.

And so he came, and watched, and dwelled.

One day, after more days than he could count, he caught the boy's sidelong glance as he ran past. The boy had his sword arm raised high, blocking his face, but he ducked his head below just long enough to look.

The man winked in greeting.

The boy turned away so quickly he stumbled, tripping over his own feet and landing face down into the sand. The sword flew a few feet farther, sticking point first.

The man lifted the heavy duffle bag in one hand and rushed to the boy's aid. The boy had already righted himself, so the man rescued the sword and brought it to the youth.

"Thank you."

"Are you okay?"

"I'm always okay." The boy flashed his big toothy grin to prove his point.

"I see you here each day," the man said.

"I see you too," the boy said. "You don't want to be here."

"It's complicated," the man said. He shifted the straps to his other hand, relieving a pain in his shoulder.

"What's in the bag?" the boy asked.

"Just some personal items."

"It looks heavy." The boy continued to eye it, his face scrunching up in thought. "I'll show you mine if you show me yours," he said after some time.

"You have something to show me?"

"My treasure," the boy said, beaming with pride. "It's

special, and hidden. I'll show you my treasure if you show me yours."

The man had nothing else to do, and he enjoyed the boy's simple exuberance.

"Deal. But you show me yours first." He extended his hand, and the boy pirate shook it, squeezing as hard as he could.

"This way!" the boy shouted, running off down the coast, his wooden sword waving in the air.

The man walked a great distance, his progress slowed by the weighty bag.

The boy ran ahead, leaving serpentine paths in the damp sand. Every once in a while the boy circled around him, telling him it wasn't much farther, but he never stayed for long, charging away again.

The burden he carried threatened to pull him down, to make him give up, but he pushed on—for the sake of the boy's excitement more than his own need.

Over time the smooth beach turned rocky, with the dry land rising above as looming cliffs. He could not say how far or long he traveled. His progress slowed on the beach as his steps became cautious and his way often blocked by boulders.

The boy, of course, climbed and jumped with grace and speed.

"How much longer?" he asked.

"Not much," the boy said.

Waves crashed against the craggy landscape, drenching his clothes and threatening to drag him out into the depths. Now soaked through, the bag dragged like an anchor behind him. He clawed his way over great stones, scrambling around deep pools hidden between the giant rocks. Exhausted and sore, he stopped in the crevasse of two boulders.

"No more." His words were nearly swallowed by the roar of the waves.

"Here we are." The boy pointed into the darkness of the crevasse, a black hollow that suggested a deeper cave. "Come and see." He slipped through.

The man heaved the bag a couple feet ahead of him and took a step. He repeated this process—heave, step, heave, step—all the way into the cave. It took a while for his eyes to adjust, but they did, revealing a narrow scar that split deep into the cliffs. Water glistened along the rock walls, and a small stream trickled out to the coast.

Half-buried in sand, a skull and ribcage poked out of the ground. The back of the skull had shattered—a flintlock fired at close range. A tarnished cutlass stuck out of the ribs.

"That's mine," the boy said from behind.

The man did not turn, but continued to study the scene. Finally he asked, "How long ago?"

"I don't know time. I only remember playing here, along the beach."

The man nodded. He realized the boy did not wish to discuss how he had died. He only wanted to show the outcome.

"It's your turn," the boy said.

The man nodded again, lifting the bag up next to the skeleton. With one hand he held a strap of the handle, and with the other he worked the zipper loose.

Inside sat several heavy rocks and a thick chain, enough to bind a man and drag him to the depths of the ocean.

"Wow . . . ." The boy's voice trailing off with a sense of awe.

The man nodded a third time, looking away from the duffle bag. He had no more desire to discuss his situation than had the boy.

"You can let go," the boy said. "Leave it here. We can go out and play."

"I . . . I can't." He held the strap tight in his fist, wrapped around once for a more secure hold.

"It's not going to help you anymore."

His head sagged to his chest. "But it's the only thing I have left." He said this to the ground, to the bag in his hands, and to his past self.

"And that's why you should let go. But what do I know? I'm just a boy." He winked at the man, covered the eye with the patch, and charged out of the cave with his sword held high.

* * * * *

He sat on a bench overlooking the ocean, watching everything but the endless waves. He abhorred the picturesque seascape, the vast horizon and the promise of the black depths below it. Still, he sat, day after day.

Each afternoon, a boy emerged from down the coast. He ran along the sand, slashing and cursing at imaginary foes. As he passed, he winked at the man.

Each time his hand twitched to rise, to return the greeting, but the hand clutched tight to the straps of a duffle bag. He did not know why the bag was so important to hold onto, but he thought perhaps one day he'd leave it there and run after the boy.

One day.

About the Author:

Bear Weiter is an illustrator, animator, artist, and writer. His fiction appears in a number of magazines and anthologies including *Black Static*, *Rigor Amortis,* and *Slices of Flesh*. Many previous works were under the pen names Jacob Ruby and Virginia Ray, but he has finally decided to brand everything under one identity—his own.

You can follow him on Twitter @bearthw or his personal site: http://www.bearweiter.com.

"Bobby's got a birthday due and there'll be a party, too."

by David Ritchey

With these words the invitation promised a great party for most of the first-grade students at The Renven Neighborhood School. The return address on the envelope indicated this party would be in one of the most exclusive neighborhoods in Renven. The guest could expect a well-organized party, great food and games, and treats for everyone.

"Chuck, this has to be the best party of the year. These parties set the standard for the next twelve years. Bobby has to be a class leader," Beth said. Her face seemed to light up with a big smile framed by her long black hair.

"Beth, I told you I'd help you with the party. What do you want me to do?" Chuck replied. Chuck Riley was taller than most men, about 6'4" and with plenty of salt-and-pepper colored hair. They were a beautiful couple, and Bobby promised to be the best of each of his parents. But, Bobby was shy. Beth hoped to free him of his quiet tendency by giving him an elaborate birthday party. He would only be seven-years old. But Beth thought you could never start too soon.

"Help me. Make sure everything is perfect. You could find some special entertainment," Beth said. "Get something the kids will remember through their senior year. We have to make sure Bobby is a success in school—and I don't mean just grades."

"How many guests?" Chuck asked.

"We're only inviting the children of the A-List parents. So, we'll have about 20 kids."

The party would be in Beth and Chuck's big tutor-style

house. They arranged valet parking. That permitted the guests to stroll up the long brick walkway to the solid-cherry front door. Flowers lined the walkway and at the door. The guests were greeted by Beth's housekeeper, Connie.

Beth had instructed Connie to take the gifts from the guests at the front door and put them on a table in the living room. "I need to keep a record of what each family brings," she said. "When those children have a birthday party we'll need gifts that are equal in value to what they gave Bobby. And, in truth, we can re-gift some of the presents."

"Parents at the adult bar," Beth announced when the guests started arriving. "Boys and girls, let's gather on the patio."

A man carrying a gym bag joined the group of adults walking to the house. "I'm Marlowe, the pirate. Or, I will be Marlowe when I get into my makeup and costume," the man said to Connie with a laugh.

Connie imaged this handsome man as a pirate. Even through his shirt, she could see his rippling muscles. She smiled, knowing she'd see Marlowe do his pirate act.

"Just a moment," Connie said. "I'll get Mr. Riley."

Chuck saw the man approach and hurried to him. "Let me take you upstairs to a bedroom where you can put on your makeup and costume and do whatever else you like to do." Chuck laughed. He placed a hand on the other man's back to direct him to the bedroom.

As they walked through the house, up the stairs and to the bedroom, Connie watched. Those guys should be best friends, she thought.

Chuck led Marlowe-to-be to a room with an adjoining bathroom. He closed the bedroom door.

"OK, won't take me long—about thirty minutes to become Marlowe, the pirate," the man said, slipping out of his shirt and tossing it on the bed.

Chuck took a clothes hanger from the closet and carefully placed the shirt on the hanger.

The man pulled off his shoes and socks and dropped his pants to the floor. His body was a weight-lifter's wedge—broad shoulders and a narrow waist. Chuck placed his hands on Marlowe's neck and started massaging him.

"That feels good. But, let's wait until later. I've got to become your neighborhood pirate."

Chuck squeezed Marlowe's shoulder and left the room. "In about 30 minutes, Marlowe, the pirate, will be here to entertain," Chuck said to his wife.

Connie served a chocolate cake with thick, rich icing. She had 15 flavors of ice cream for the children. The bartender at the adult bar continued to serve the parents.

"Best party, ever," Beth whispered to Chuck.

Marlowe walked out onto the patio. He wore black shoes and a skin-tight pair of red pants and a black, pirate-style shirt. His wig complemented his fake black beard. He wore a large, black patch over his left eye.

The kids gasped with pleasure when they saw him. They had seen the pirate movies, and here was a real-life pirate at Bobby's birthday party. The children joined their parents in applauding for Marlowe.

Beth could not have been happier.

"OK, boys and girls, I want to start with a trick that will require your help. Bobby, since you're the birthday boy, come up and help me."

Bobby glanced at Chuck and indicated he didn't want to participate in the clown's act. "Oh, come on Bobby, be a good sport," his father said.

Bobby stood beside the pirate.

"What's going to happen is that I'm going to make Bobby disappear. This is my favorite party trick."

Marlowe had a series of large metal hoops about two-feet across. These circles were linked together by black velvet. In some ways this prop looked like a big, black velvet worm. Marlowe smiled at the guests. "I want you to help me. We'll count backwards from three to one: THREE, TWO, ONE. OK, let's practice: THREE, TWO, ONE. OK." Marlowe and the children counted together—"THREE, TWO, ONE."

Marlowe placed the hoops over Bobby. He slowly pulled the top ring up so that Bobby was complete encircles by the black velvet and the metal circles.

"OK, this is it for real—THREE, TWO, ONE." Marlowe and the children counted, and at one, Marlowe let the metal hoops fall and Bobby had disappeared.

The children gasped. The parents applauded. Beth smiled with pleasure and then looked to Chuck.

Everyone expected Marlowe to make Bobby appear. Marlowe lifted the rings. Nothing happened. The children expected Bobby to appear from behind a tree, from under a patio table or, maybe, from behind the bar. Marlowe stepped from the patio and went into the house.

Beth barely kept her composure. "Chuck, find Marlowe. Tell him the game is over. He needs to bring Bobby back."

The children's silence suggested that they would never forget this party. Beth looked around the backyard. "Where is Bobby?" she whispered to Chuck.

"I don't know," he said. "I thought you'd talked to the pirate before he started his act."

"No," Beth shouted. "The entertainment was your responsibility. You messed up again."

Chuck ran into the house and charged up the stairs to the bedroom where Marlowe changed his clothes.

Not only had Bobby disappeared, so had Marlowe.

The party ended. Connie gently led the guests to the door.

Beth called the police. She had difficulty explaining on the phone that a pirate had made her son disappear at a birthday party. Finally, the police arrive, and Beth and Chuck tried to make the police officers understand what had happened. The police wanted to question Marlowe, but they couldn't find him.

Beth went to her bedroom and laid on the bed. She closed

her eyes and felt tears flow from her eyes and down her cheek. "Bobby, Bobby," she whispered.

"Mommy, I'm here."

"Bobby, where are you?" Beth screamed.

"I'm here on the ceiling. The pirate did something to me. I can't get back to being myself."

"Bobby, Bobby . . . stay there a moment. All I can see is a small shadow darting around."

"Chuck, Chuck," Beth screamed. "Come here, Chuck."

* * * * *

"Chuck, Chuck," Marlowe said in another part of town, "It's good to lie here with you." Marlowe had removed most of his pirate makeup. He ran his fingers down Chuck's nude back. "It's over?"

"Yes," said Chuck. "I've grown to hate Beth. Bobby's disappearance will push her over the top. You can expect to see her in the psychiatric ward any day now."

"What about Bobby?" Marlowe asked.

"He was her kid from a previous relationship. I never did like him. Good riddance."

Marlowe caressed Chuck's well-formed butt.

"I have only one question," Chuck said. "How did you do it?"

Marlowe smiled, "Magic. Pure pirate magic."

About the Author:

David Ritchey is the theater critic for *The West Side Leader* in Akron, Ohio, and a member of the American Association of Theater Critics. Ritchey is a Professor in the School of Communication at The University of Akron.

Ritchey attended the Breadloaf Writers' Conference in Vermont and he participated in Scotland's Hawthornden Castle Writers' Retreat.

He has taught in Beijing, Hong Kong; Bucharest and

London. He consulted for the US government in St. Petersburg, Russia, and visited Cuba.

In 2003, he was a Senior Fulbright Scholar in Romania.

Retirees In Space

by Anne Marie Lutz

When Grun heard the shout from the main cabin, at first she thought Mike was watching another ball game. The man tended to get loud when he watched football, no matter that the games were old ones, long decided, transmitted to them after they had exited hyperspace. The man would turn on the vid in the main cabin and bellow at the teams as if he were still on Earth and the players could actually hear him.

Then she heard it again, and it was definitely a scream.

Grun leaped up from the pilot's chair. She caught herself before she snapped the order to transfer command to a junior officer. Old habits died hard, and it was easy to forget this was a luxury yacht, in port on Forst, not the hard metal deck of the *Defender*.

She slammed through the hatch into the passenger cabins, her hand on the grip of her energy weapon.

Mike was backed up against the bulkhead, his usually-florid face drained of color. His wife, Hi, stood before him, wearing her silk pajamas. An odd lump bulged under the neck of her pajama top.

Grun squinted at it, unsure what was going on.

Mike saw her. "Kill it!" His voice rose, broke.

"No!" Hi shouted. She held up her hands, palms out, toward Grun. "Put it away, put the gun away!"

The odd lump wiggled, shifting the collar of Hi's robe in a shimmering pattern. Something almost transparent moved, tinged with tendrils of pink, like blood dissipating in clear water.

"Holy hell!" Grun recognized it from the tour of the planet. The things were supposed to be contained, locked up behind a force field in a sanctuary where they could do no harm. Now here was an actual alien parasite on little Hi's neck. Grun looked around for something to use, to pry the obscene thing from Hi's body.

"Grun, stop. I am all right." Hi did not appear to be wounded or dying.

Grun blinked.

If anything, Hi appeared exasperated. "Would you quit your shrieking, Michael? We'll have the others in here."

Grun hesitated. She kept the gun trained on the alien. She could never risk killing Hi, but if the creature moved Grun would be ready. Voices came from behind her as the remaining occupants of the yacht filed into the cabin.

"Before you send it into defense mode, don't panic!" Hi said.

"My God, you've done it again, woman," Mike growled. His voice had descended to its usual register. He slid along the bulkhead, reaching for the drink he'd left on the table. "I need a drink. What have you done now?"

Iker's dignified head peered around the corner. He blanched and dropped the *Interplanetary Markets* he had been reading. "Jesus, Hi. What have you gone and done? Does the ambassador know? Milla, look what Hi has gone and liberated from the planet."

Milla shrieked. "Hi, get it off you!"

Iker held his wife's arm close. "She did it on purpose, Mill. I don't know why."

Milla's voice shook. "I don't approve, Hi. There's a reason those things have been kept isolated for the last fifty years. Remember that awful infestation, behind the containment walls? What do they say about Earthers barging into other worlds' affairs, as if we think we always know best?"

"Oh, Milla, don't worry. I'll explain. I promise I didn't steal it to make a point."

"I hope not, Hi." Grun had gotten the idea there was no immediate danger and put her gun away. Her nerves still thrummed with battle-readiness. She was hired to be a pilot for Mama's retired friends, earning some money while she recovered from her wounds. But it was perfectly clear, if unspoken, that Grun would be the last line of defense for these civilians should it be needed. She wished she knew if it were needed.

The alien still pulsed on Hi's neck. It didn't seem to be growing any redder, and Hi was behaving just as Hi usually did— just now earnestly describing to Milla how unfairly the aliens had been treated.

"Imprisoned on their own planet, Milla!" Hi argued. "They're on a reservation, kept from communicating outside the walls, and kept from their only decent source of nutrients—"

"Us!" roared Mike. "Go on all you like about unfairness. What were we supposed to do, let them eat us?"

Hi frowned at him. "They can eat any warm-blooded creature, Mike. They simply *prefer* more evolved life." One hand went up to touch the alien's skin. It dimpled slightly with the pressure of her fingers, like soft plastic filled with gel.

Grun shuddered.

"She means it isn't our planet, Mike," Iker said. He drew closer to Hi, his feet in rich slippers scuffing a little on the carpeted deck. "I assume the thing has eaten recently?"

"Seems so," Grun said. "It's apparently not hungry."

"I'm perfectly safe," Hi said. "The ambassador promised. And this creature is going to help us get the drop on the pirates."

* * * * *

Grun snapped a final acknowledgement to Forst Control and slammed a hand down on the communications console. "They're refusing us clearance to return. Hi set us up!" she said to Iker.

"No surprise there." Iker sat beside her with his slippered feet stretched out before him, lounging in the copilot's seat as if he were in his den on Earth. "Hi is a force to be reckoned with."

"I thought she was timid." Grun turned her head, listening. There was no sound from the main cabin, where Mike was standing guard over Hi with Grun's energy gun in one hand and a stiff drink in the other.

Iker sat looking at the vastness of space.

"Well, we can't return to Forst and offload this thing," Grun said. "I wonder if we can pry it off her and fling it out the main lock?"

"I think Hi would resist us. And who knows what the creature would do in such a case?"

Grun shuddered. "What do we know about these aliens, anyway?" She scanned the displays. Everything was green for departure. The yacht's expensive drive hummed. Grun tapped in a code and stood.

"Oh, don't go without me." Iker rose with measured grace. He drew a hand through his silver hair and smiled, as if nothing that happened here disturbed him very much. "I want to be there for this."

Hi sat at the table in the main cabin, drinking hot chocolate. The alien curled around her neck gleamed clear-and-pink.

Mike wavered in front of her. He brandished the energy weapon at Hi. "I don't wanna have to do this," he said. "But I will. Because I love you, that's why."

Grun grabbed the weapon and put it back in the holster at her belt. "Enough of that. Sit down. Where's Milla?"

The other woman walked back into the cabin. "What's happening?" She took hold of Iker's arm and clung. Iker patted her ringed fingers and looked at Grun, for all the world, as if he expected her to entertain him.

Grun sighed. "We can't return to Forst. They've refused permission."

"What if we return anyway?" Milla asked. "What do you think they would do? We're just a group of old people on vacation. Can Forst afford to antagonize Earth by taking action against us?"

"There's always Surra," Hi said.

"They say those pirates use Surra. It's off the itinerary as of last week. They've even played havoc with Forst's routes," Iker said.

"Someone needs to do something about it. Did you notice how empty everything was down there?" Hi asked. "The temples, the alien catacombs, even the gambling halls? Forst is a rich planet, but only because of people like us."

"Tourists, young rich people on wanderjahr, retired people with money," Iker said.

"No one was there. The pirates are preying on Forst's lifeblood. They want them caught." Hi stroked the alien with her forefinger. Grun wondered if there was more pink in its gut than there had been before. But Hi seemed perfectly all right.

"So send out a warship!" Mike blustered. "Who does that ambassador think we are?"

"Warships have done no good," Iker said. "I was speaking with an old business acquaintance who retired here. The pirates don't bother the warships, or even the smaller ships sent out to chase them down. Somehow they know what ships to hit. Stock in Forst's pleasure industry is down by half since we left Merrose III."

"Damn their money, this is my wife!" Mike said. Grun had been despising him, but at that she felt her expression soften.

Hi reached out a hand to Mike. "My dear, all is well if we simply do as I have agreed."

"And what's that?" Grun said. "If you'll pardon me, we have to choose a course. Forst is forbidding us docking privileges. We have to go. I could set a course back to Earth, but—"

"No, no!" Hi said. "It takes too long. The alien will have to eat by then."

Even Iker went pale at that.

"All right," Grun said slowly. "I suppose that means we head to Merrose III, where the authorities can—"

"No, no!" Hi protested. "We'll go where we intended to go, to see the rainbow cliffs of Surra before they fall into the chasm."

"Honey, we aren't exactly on vacation anymore," Milla said.

She reached out to pat Hi's hand. The creature around Hi's neck stirred for the first time, a pulsing motion stilled in the blink of an eye. Milla pulled back her hand fast.

"I said we would."

"Without consulting anyone?" Grun shook her head. "I know I'm just the pilot."

"It is just like her, dear," Iker said. "I am sorry we've put you in this position. Best go set a course for Surra."

"We're going to take down the space pirates, with *one* alien parasite?" Mike asked. His eyes showed white around the irises. Grun wondered how he had been married to Hi for so long and not expected something like this. But then, they had never been retired in space before, with no obligations to anyone but themselves. Perhaps Hi was different here than she had been at home, with her tech job in the city and her children.

"I don't think it'll come to that," Grun said. "I'll get us as close to Surra as possible on the jump. They can't interfere with us in hyperspace, you know, and the jump coordinates are closely patrolled to protect against just this sort of thing. Unless Surra is actively involved with the pirates, we'll be safe there. Then we can figure out what to do with the alien without hurting Hi."

* * * * *

Somehow, Grun was not surprised when the ship's sensors blared a warning and dropped them out of hyperspace into the vastness between the stars. She hit the intraship comm. "We're in normal space. Verifying our location. I'd prepare for problems if I were all of you."

"Forced out of hyperspace? I thought that was impossible." Milla's voice shook.

Grun didn't blame her at all. "I don't see how. The route is well mapped. The drive was just maintained. There are no anomalies that would—" A readout blinked red on the console, and Grun's mouth twisted. "Unless, of course, Forst uploaded something to drop us out. The computer is saying it received programming while we were docked."

"Those sneaky bastards!" Milla's voice shook. "The pirates have an ally in Forst Control! Wait until I tell the ambassador. He's never really gotten over me; he'll nail that spy to the wall for me!" She twisted one carefully curled strand of hair in nervous fingers.

Grun told the ship's computer to fire on the attacking vessel. There was no response but a series of flashing yellow lights. "Guns are unavailable," Grun said. "Guess they disabled those, too."

A red light flashed. "Proximity warning." Grun hit the comm again. "Here they come!" She locked down the helm, put the hailing channel on comm and stood up, loosening her energy gun in its holster.

Milla vanished into the living quarters.

"Let us in, little piggy," said a voice through the comm. "Give us what we want, and there'll be no one hurt."

Hi stood before the table in the main cabin, Mike flushed with tension and drink at her side. Iker and Milla were nowhere to be seen.

"Yes, let them in!" Mike said. "We'll give them our money, and they'll let us go on to Surra. My company can send us cash there."

Milla poked her head out of her sleeping quarters. "Don't listen. They'll kill us and take the ship. Didn't you pay any attention to the news while we were on Forst?"

The ship rocked to an impact off the bow. An alarm beeped on the bridge, transmitted over the ship's comm. Grun winced.

"Let us in, sweet little yacht," said the voice from the hailing frequency. "I won't hesitate to blow a hole in you if you don't let us dock. No loss for us, after all." The voice hardened. "Let us in. Five minutes."

Grun looked at Hi. She appeared as calm as ever. Hi had drawn her collar up to cover the alien. If you didn't know what you were looking for, you would never know the horror she kept around her neck.

"I don't know what the plan is," Grun said to Hi. "But get ready. Our weapons are unavailable, and we have no choice."

Hi nodded.

"Holy God," Mike said.

"Go in the cabin, dear," Hi told Mike.

The red-faced man shook his head. "Not leavin' you, Hi."

Hi's face softened. Then she nodded at Grun. "Open the lock."

Grun ordered systems to open the outer lock. The computer warned they were in deep space—"Confirmation requested"—and Grun overrode the safety.

"That's more like it," said the voice from the pirate vessel. "I'll see you in just a moment. I'm warning you, we have plenty of weapons, and we'll take out any of ya who lifts a gun to us. Be smart now." The channel closed.

It seemed forever while the lock cycled through. Grun flattened her back against the inner hull next to the airlock, sighting along her outstretched arm to her drawn energy gun. Still, she was undecided. Should she shoot and kill as many of the bastards as she could before they killed her? What good would that do the others? Tactics streaked through her mind as she waited. Then she shrugged to herself and squinted along the gunsight. She would not let Mama's retired friends be taken without a fight.

The readout showed the lock was occupied. The pressure crept upward. Grun heard a sob from the direction of Iker and Milla's cabin. The muscles in her side twinged where she had been wounded in her last action. Then the airlock hushed open.

Grun sighted, but no one came through the lock. Instead, a round metal thing rolled, fast, out on the deck. *Grenade*, Grun thought, then *No . . . not in a pressurized cabin.* As she stared after it, someone rounded the corner of the airlock, crouched to waist level, and fired at Grun. Bright light flashed in Grun's eyes. Massive sound breached her eardrums. Blackness folded over her eyes, and she fell before she could fire at the boarding party.

* * * * *

Hearing returned first. Familiar voices—Milla's frightened tones, strained with tears, and Mike's blustery objections to something. The carpet on the deck—carpet! On a ship's deck! That was Iker's conceit—scratched at Grun's arm. Then awareness returned, and Grun barely stopped herself from rolling and grabbing for her gun.

Still, she must have moved. A foot prodded at her.

"Your pet soldier is awake," a voice said. It was the same voice she had heard on the comm from the pirate ship. Grun blinked and sat up, coiled and ready. Her eyes searched for her energy gun and found it on the deck across the cabin. There were three strangers in the cabin, and one of them had a blaster aimed directly at Grun's forehead.

The post-stun headache pounded behind Grun's eyes. She was surprised they hadn't just killed her—perhaps they had a use for a pilot.

"Don't move," said the voice, lilting with a spark that led Grun to think this was a man who loved what he did for the thrill of it. His dark eyes betrayed an unexpected humor as he stared down at her. His black, military-style boot rested on her ribs.

"I want up," she said.

He nodded. "Slowly." He backed off a little, blaster ready. Grun rose with a slowness born of caution and also of her aching ribs.

Hi, Milla and Iker sat at the table, under guard. Mike lay on the deck, out cold. The pirate leader saw her watching Mike and said: "He's alive. Old fool tried to jump me. Might have done it thirty years ago, but not today."

The rest of the cabin was in a shambles. Storage compartments spewed supplies everywhere. A bag of emergency rations had split open, trailing algae meal down the side of the bulkhead. As Grun watched, there was a thump from one of the sleeping cabins and someone inside threw a ball of rolled-up clothing out into the passageway.

"Nothing here, Jay!" yelled a woman's voice from the sleeping cabin. She put her head out the hatch to glare at Grun's pirate. "Not so much as a gold bracelet. Waste of time!"

"Not like we were gonna do anything else," Jay said. He scratched at the stubble on his jaw. "Where's the cash then, folks? People your age don't run around between star systems with just cereal and a few extra clothes, do ya now? Where's the cash? Where's the prescription drugs? I know ya've got 'em."

Iker said, "I could pay you to leave us alone."

"Now you've got the idea." Jay waved his blaster at Iker, who seemed unmoved. Grun tensed, but one of the other pirates growled, "Don't move," at her.

"You," Jay said. His eyes narrowed at Iker. "Get up. Show us the safe."

Iker nodded. "It's in the sleeping cabin."

Milla sobbed and clutched at his arm. "He's just going to kill us and take the ship anyway!"

The woman in Milla's room said, "Don't trust us, do you? Sad. Send him in, Jay. You're a handsome old man, aren't you? Must've been a looker when you were young?" She held a gun steady as Iker and Milla preceded her into the sleeping cabin.

Grun's mind twisted through scenario after scenario. She wondered if they would really just take the money and go, leaving this expensive little space yacht behind them. She didn't think so. After the passengers had given away the location of any safes or secret compartments, she thought they would be tossed out the airlock so the pirates could take over.

She saw the exact moment when Jay's dark gaze fixed on Hi.

"You," he said. "What's that around your neck?"

"Nothing." Hi appeared sharp and alert. Grun recognized that look from combat training. Hi was ready for anything.

"Nothing, hell. You've got something good there. What is it, a special necklace? Hand it over." The pirate stalked over to the table and put a hand at Hi's silk collar and pulled it aside. "Shit!"

The alien rippled from Hi's neck, lightning fast. It flowed up onto Jay's wrist before the pirate could let go of Hi's collar. It stretched, elongated, encased Jay's hand, wrist, and forearm.

The pirate leaped back. "Holy hell, what is it? Get it off!" He dropped his energy gun, trying to peel the alien off with his other hand. In just seconds, it glistened in a mucous mass up from Jay's neck to his mouth.

Everyone was watching Jay. Grun scrambled across the deck, grabbed her energy gun and got off one blast at one of the pirates. The man dropped dead before he sprawled to the deck. The other pirate swore and fired. Fire seared the edge of Grun's arm, burning up her shoulder. The arm fell limp, but she was still alive. She squeezed the trigger one more time and the other shooter screamed and crashed to the deck.

Blackness tinged Grun's vision, but she could still see that Jay had collapsed. He was enveloped in a sleeve of clear-and-rose alien, which had somehow grown and thinned to cover his entire body. Jay thrashed. His face through the distorting film of the alien's body was purpling with hypoxia and grotesque as he fought uselessly against something that gave with his every blow.

Iker walked out of his cabin. There was no sign of the pirate he had gone in with. "This one's dead," he said. His voice seemed just as calm as usual. "I have her gun. Shall I—?"

"Shoot," Grun forced out. She could no longer see clearly enough to shoot. In fact, she was not sure she was even holding her weapon. "Kill it."

Iker raised the weapon.

Hi sprung to her feet and leapt between Iker and the fallen pirate. "No, no! Leave it alone!"

Milla emerged from the sleeping cabin and sank to her knees at Grun's side. Through the haze of faintness that cushioned her perception, Grun noticed that Milla was smeared with blood. The older woman held one of the emergency med kits. After a moment's fumbling with wrappers and seals, Milla administered an injection of the pain medication. Then she wrapped a cool gel bandage around Grun's forearm. After a moment of almost indescribable relief, Grun's thoughts sharpened. "Why not kill it, while it's uh, otherwise occupied?" she gritted out to Hi.

"Because that's not part of the deal! It won't hurt us now. It has what it wants."

"Holy God," Mike grumbled as he sat up, holding his head. "What in hell can it *want*, Hi? And I never thought about divorce before, I swear I didn't, but after this day—"

"I love you, too," Hi said. She bent over the twisting form of the alien-encased pirate. The man's face had turned almost black.

Grun spared a moment's hazy regret for the loss—he had been a beauty—but then wrenched herself back to reality.

"What does it want, Hi," Milla pleaded. "Tell us for God's sake!"

"Genetic material," Hi said. "Human DNA. And not ours, it agreed, and not from the humans on Forst or the tourists it depends on."

"What in hell is it going to do with human DNA?"

Hi stood up and took a deep breath, as if she were letting go of stress. She rubbed the skin of her neck and shoulder. When her hand came away, Grun saw her skin speckled with little dots, each one a clotted tiny wound where the alien had clung.

"It took your blood," Iker said. "It had your DNA. Why go to this extreme?" he gestured at Jay, who had fallen still.

"The alien swore to the ambassador it would not hurt me, but it has to have some means of staying alive." Hi drew her silk collar over the abraded skin. "I am fine. It took nothing but a little blood."

"But what does it need to consume that pirate for?"

"DNA," Hi said. She sounded impatient, and finally a little shell-shocked. "Its species needs the DNA. It will take it back to Forst, to the containment zone."

Mike put a beefy arm around her shoulders. "Leave her alone now. Can't you see, she's exhausted?"

"We're stranded." Iker looked at Grun. "Is there anything you can do about the navigation or communications back to Forst?"

Grun nodded. "Now that I have time." The gel pack and the shot had dulled the pain. She felt lightheaded from the drug, but there was no choice. She accepted Iker's help back to the helm. The first thing she did was scan for the pirate craft, but sensors showed nothing nearby.

"Huh," Grun said. "I think they left someone aboard, and they scrammed as soon as they realized there were problems."

"Just as well," Iker said. "Here, Milla has brought some hot tea for you."

Grun sipped it and winced. It was loaded with sugar, cloying on her tongue. "I don't like—"

"I know. But you need it right now. Where will we be if you faint, and we're left here with no comm or propulsion in the middle of nothing?"

"Hi knows how to work the comm," Grun said. "Mike knows something about the drive." A few minutes later, she had figured out what the accomplice at Forst Control had done to their ship. She entered code to free the comm. As soon as she began sending their location and a mayday, the comm spat a stream of gibberish that resolved into a frantic voice. It did not sound like the voice of Forst Control.

"Forst Control to Ramblin' Days—"

"This is Ramblin' Days." Grun winced again at the name Mike had saddled the little yacht with.

"Forst Control to Milla. Where is Milla?"

Grun laughed. "Must be the ambassador. The old boyfriend," she said to Iker. Then: "This is Captain Grun. We are fine, need a little medical attention but all are well. We need assistance in debugging our nav computer and yeah, also in transporting some dead pirates."

There was a babble of confused voices and Forst Control came back online, cool and professional. "Pinpointing your location and sending rescue. What is the status of the pirate vessel?"

"Gone, but we have four of them here, three deceased and one on storage," Grun said. She raised her eyebrows at Iker, who shrugged. He didn't know what to say about Jay either.

"Warning to Forst Control," Grun added. "The pirates had planetside assistance. Someone capable of uploading course changes and weapons programming from Forst Control." More than likely they'd done it themselves in order to appease the alien parasites and to kill a few pirates, but the diplomatic approach seemed prudent, now that Grun needed their help.

After the flurry of acknowledgments, Grun locked down the helm and went back to the main cabin. The pirate leader lay like some grotesque biology experiment on the deck, but someone had pushed him off to the side. Hi and Mike sat close together on the couch, and Milla's voice contributed a jittery background as she ran through her feelings about the pirate attack, trying to relieve her stress.

"Milla, come here," Iker said. "Enough now, you can tell the officers later."

"They damn well better honor Hi as a hero of Forst," Mike blustered, a drink in his hand. "She saved the alien species!"

"By helping them evolve, yes, dear," Hi said.

"And funding a day at the casinos. That would be a nice mark of appreciation as well, don't you think?" Iker said. "Milla rather likes the slots."

Hi yawned behind one delicate hand. "Now I think I am very tired, and Grun needs to sit down. Would someone get my origami kit? Will you, Iker? I find it calms my nerves, to focus on detail."

Iker bowed. "At your service."

Grun settled with her feet up and the voices of her passengers droning in her ears—about origami, Iker thinking out what this would do to the tourist industry on Forst and the price of stock, and Mike looking for a vid of a football game in the locker under the couch, which had somehow escaped being looted. Grun smiled. Heroes of Forst, indeed. All ready for a nice meal, after the rescue ship came, and perhaps a nip of something before bed.

About the Author:

Anne Marie has always loved reading (and writing!), especially in the genres of science fiction and fantasy. She holds a Bachelor of Arts degree in Journalism and an MBA, both from the Ohio State University. She has worked as an office manager, an operations analyst and more recently at home raising her children.

Anne Marie enjoys reading, spending time with friends and family, and traveling when she can.

Anne Marie was raised in the Youngstown area. She lives in Central Ohio with her husband and their two children. Her new novel in the Color Mage series titled, *Sword of Jashan*, is due out in September 2013.

www.loconeal.com

loconeal.com/category/locoblog

www.facebook.com/LoconealPublishing

Breaking News

Forthcoming Releases

Links to Author Sites

Loconeal Events